ARRIVEDERCI MILLWALL
and
SMALLHOLDINGS

ARRIVEDERCI
MILLWALL
and
SMALLHOLDINGS

NICK PERRY

faber and faber
LONDON · BOSTON

First published in 1987
by Faber and Faber Limited
3 Queen Square London WC1N 3AU

Photoset by Wilmaset Birkenhead Wirral
Printed in Great Britain by
Redwood Burn Ltd Trowbridge Wiltshire
All rights reserved

All rights whatsoever in this play are
strictly reserved and application for
performance, etc., should be made before
rehearsal to Rochelle Stevens & Co,
15–17 Islington High Street, London N1 1LQ.

British Library Cataloguing in Publication Data

Perry, Nick
Arrivederci Millwall and smallholdings.
I. Title
822'.914   PR6066.E7/
ISBN 0–571–14774–7

CONTENTS

ARRIVEDERCI MILLWALL

CHARACTERS

BILLY JARVIS

CASS

MAL

KENNO

TERRY

HARRY KELLERWAY

BOBBY JARVIS

OLDER MAN (in Portsmouth bar)

PADRE (Ian Mellor)

MAN FROM LEEDS (Paratrooper)

KNIGHT

KING

PARA

PEASANT

PC MARDINER

MARIO

COOK

PRIEST

MOUNTED POLICEMAN

POLICEMAN (outside football ground)

NORTHERNER

TANNOY VOICE

JOHN NOTT

TRAMP

NCO

SPANISH WAITER

SPANISH COP

and MPs, RATINGS, MARINES, SAILORS, SOLDIERS, SPANIARDS, STATUES and the GHOST, played by members of the company

Arrivederci Millwall was first performed at the Albany Empire, Deptford, London, on 18 October 1985. The cast was as follows:

BILLY JARVIS	Jonathan Moore
CASS, PARA	Eamonn Walker
MAL, MAN FROM LEEDS (Paratrooper), KNIGHT, NCO	Frank Harper
KENNO, KING, TRAMP	Nick Conway
TERRY, PEASANT, JOHN NOTT	Stuart Wilde
HARRY KELLERWAY, OLDER MAN, PADRE	Stephen Marcus
BOBBY JARVIS, PC MARDINER, MARIO, PRIEST, NORTHERNER, SPANISH WAITER, SPANISH COP	Roger Monk

Director	Teddy Kiendl
Assistant director	Shaila Parthasarathi
Designer	Paddy Kamara
Lighting design	Jack Linstrum and Matt Shadder

FIRST HALF

BILLY: (*Sings:*)
> When I was just a little boy
> I asked my mummy, what will it be?
> Will it be Arsenal, will it be Spurs?
> Here's what she said to me:

THE LADS: (*Chant:*)
> MILLWALL MILLWALL
> MILLWALL MILLWALL MILLWALL
> MILLWALL MILLWALL MILLWALL
> MILLWALL MILLWALL

BILLY: (*To the audience*) First it's one thing then it's another thing. Before you know it, it's something else. You got to stay wise, know what I mean? Everything's a fashion. Clothes. Cars. Weapons. Yeah, weapons and all. When my old man – (God rest his soul) – was my age, it was the dance hall, the broken bottle. Today it's what? The Stanley knife. That's progress for you.

But one thing you can rely on: London's always first. And first is first, second's nowhere. London talks, England walks. South London to be exact. Am I right? How can you tell a Londoner? Easy. He's fifteen times smarter than all the rest. Argies start at Calais, civilization ends at Watford. You better believe it.

Remember the sporting look? It started here, I'm proud to say. We're talking a couple, three years back now.

I think about that time a lot. Good times, they was. This was the boys. This was our life. We was sharp in them days, I tell you. We was . . . untouchable.

(*A burst of Beatbox as* MAL *hits the catwalk: rhythmic background as* BILLY *talks and* THE LADS *strut and pose the peacock male.*)

Malcolm is wearing a Tacchini track suit – (clock the label . . . North London is still wearing Lacoste, which we dropped months ago). The track suit retails at one hundred pounds – (notice the zips undone for a slight flare effect). The trainers, from Nike, fifty quid the pair. Malcolm's hair was done by Adrienne of Lewisham Hair Design Studio – in the popular 'wedgie' style. (Thank you, Malcolm.)

Kenno is wearing a soft beige combination of Armani jumper and Farrah slacks. The jacket is Burberry – (notice he wears it turned up at the cuff, to show the lining. North London is wearing them inside out, but that's North London for you.) The watch is a Rolex. The car, a Capri. (Thank you, Kenno. Love the crocs.)

Terry, showing the American influence, is wearing an original M24 copy. And underneath, in blue and white (for Millwall and Saint George) the trusty Fred Perry T-shirt. (Thank you, Tel.)

And introducing Jah Lion of New Cross Gate – Cass is wearing a plain white T-shirt (forty pounds from Cecil Gee), straight-cut Lois jeans . . . and a police helmet.
(POLICEMAN *runs on, bareheaded*.)

POLICEMAN: Oi, you!
(ALL *freeze while* BILLY *talks*.)

BILLY: PC Mardiner is wearing regulation-issue size-twelve Doctor Martens. Which went out with the fucking ark.
(ALL *unfreeze*.)

POLICEMAN: You shitting bastards!

CASS: Billy! Catch!
(CASS *throws him the helmet:* ALL *freeze*.)

BILLY: We drink our beer from the bottle and shoot some pool. Saturdays we watch Millwall play. PC Mardiner gets the overtime. It's what you might call the balance of nature.
(ALL *unfreeze*.)

POLICEMAN: I want you, Jarvis!

BILLY: Come and get it, copper! Make my fucking day!

POLICEMAN: Dog Handlers! Dog Handlers, over here!

CASS: Split!
(ALL *scatter, leaving* BILLY *alone*.)

BILLY: Looking back, I can't believe the things we did. We must of been mad. I've seen the odd newspaper clipping and I've gone: that's never me. But there it is in black and white. There's no denying it. And I'll tell you what I'm thinking. I'm thinking: what was all that fighting for? All that running, all that singing? I'll tell you. A football team. A shitty poxy wanky tenth-rate third-division fucking USELESS . . . football team.

(*Pause.*)

When you got a kid, you see things different.

(*For the first time, we see the pram.* BILLY *pushes it away.* CASS *enters in overalls, carrying paint and brushes.*)

Them days, Cass and me was partners. We was in business, painting and decorating. Our motto was: give us a slum, we'll show you a profit. We did all right.

CASS: He's give me a cheque.

BILLY: Tell him it's cash or we blowtorch the lot. These landlords they have got some front.

CASS: Did you get the mushroom?

BILLY: They only had cream.

CASS: Shit. What we gonna do?

BILLY: Mushroom, cream: what's the difference?

CASS: The colour.

BILLY: Shit, Cass. At fifty quid a day what does he expect? Fucking Rembrandt? (*To the audience*) You're in business, you do business. It's a fact of life, there's people out there, they'll rob you blind, deaf and dumb. You got to do it to them before they do it to you.

CASS: Let's get this shit on the wall.

BILLY: (*To the audience*) Everybody's at it. Only the mugs is missing out.

(CASS *tunes trannie in to Capital Radio. He and* BILLY *start to work.* KENNO *starts working his market stall.*)

KENNO: Fresh English strawberries, first of the season! Pound a punnet, one pound I'm asking! Come on, darling, don't be shy. Put your best foot forward and the worst is over. Here you are, try one, no extra charge. They might be small but so was Napoleon. Lovely, ent they? There you are, ladies – living proof. I tell you what, girls: I'm in a good mood this morning (mind your own business) – you buy two punnets I'll give you one for nothing. I can't say

7

fairer than that, can I?

(TERRY *and* HARRY *are examining a suitcase full of shirts.*)

HARRY: Feel that. Hundred per cent cotton.

TERRY: Yeah?

HARRY: Oh yes.

TERRY: How much?

HARRY: Five.

TERRY: You're shitting me.

HARRY: That's one-quarter retail value.

TERRY: Yeah?

HARRY: Oh yes. You know your chest size?

TERRY: Not offhand.

HARRY: I'll take a shot at thirty-eight. I tell you what: I give you two thirty-eights, you take the rest at five. How does that sound?

(MAL *is fly-pitching on Oxford Street.*)

MAL: Come on, ladies, gather round. What I got for you today: some genuine stolen property. I am talking top-range perfume. I've got Yves Saint Laurent at £40 a bottle. I've got Chanel at £50. I've got White Satin at £60. That's a total retail price of £150. Now I don't want £150, do I? No. I don't want £100. I don't even want half-price. Thirty pound the lot before the police come one way and my business goes the other.

BILLY: You got the time?

CASS: Quarter to.

BILLY: What day is it today?

CASS: Tuesday.

BILLY: Shit.

(ALL *hurry to pack away businesses and change out of work clothes. Then* ALL *race to form a queue at a sign reading: Box No. 23. The scene is now the dole office.* MAL *is last in.*)

MAL: Hello, boys. How's business?

(*As one, they turn and glare at him.*)

KENNO: (*Hisses*) Speak up, Malcolm. The Fraud Squad didn't hear you.

MAL: (*Whispers*) Shit. I'm sorry. I got fucking chased down Oxford Street.

8

HARRY: (*To* MAL) Borrow your paper? Ta.

MAL: (*Joining queue behind* TERRY) I got fucking chased down Oxford Street.

HARRY: (*Reading*) Aye aye. Jaguar's up six points.

TERRY: (*To* MAL) Do you know your chest size?

MAL: No.

TERRY: What I need is a tape measure.

HARRY: (*Reading*) Flash Harry's running at Catford. Sounds tempting. Anyone fancy a syndicate?

BILLY: Dogs is a fucking lottery. They ent got no form.

HARRY: You got to speculate to accumulate.

KENNO: Some of us got to work.

HARRY: Some of us is mugs then, ent we?

MAL: (*To* HARRY) Can I have my paper back?

HARRY: Hold your horses.

MAL: I ent looked at it yet.

HARRY: (*Calls*) Come on, let's have some service round here!

CASS: This ent McDonald's.

HARRY: They got the right idea, the Americans.

CASS: Then why don't you emigrate?

HARRY: I was born here, sunshine.

TERRY: (*To* MAL) Do you want to see a shirt?

MAL: No.

BILLY: (*To the audience*) Off the cards, on the lump – you name it, we was at it. We had more fiddles than Mantovani. We had so much money, we didn't know what to do with it. (*The scene is now a pool hall.* KENNO *and* TERRY *play pool.* BILLY, CASS *and* MAL *watch.*) So what's happening?

CASS: What you fancy?

BILLY: Take your pick. You seen one, you seen 'em all.

CASS: All right. Samson's.

BILLY: Except Samson's. I was about to say, except Samson's.

TERRY: You want to see my trick shot? The number five stripe in the top left pocket.

MAL: What's wrong with Samson's?

BILLY: They're just a bunch of thieving shitheads.

MAL: Fair enough.

TERRY: What we need here is plenty of screw.

KENNO: Abso–fucking–lutely.

TERRY: Quiet please. (*Plays the shot.*) Sweet.

MAL: Steve Davis, eat shit.

TERRY: You see, what it is: it's all about delivering a straight cue, innit.

KENNO: The thing is, Terry: you're spots. I'm stripes.

TERRY: Oh no.

KENNO: Foul shot.

MAL: What about Drovers?

BILLY: The wallpaper gives me headache.

KENNO: Gilly's?

BILLY: You're welcome to it. That's all I'm gonna say.

CASS: Dun Cow?

BILLY: Just fuck right off.

CASS: Why not? Make a change.

BILLY: You're joking.

CASS: No.

BILLY: You name me one good reason I should enter that piss-hole, I'll buy you a pint.

CASS: The music.

BILLY: The music.

CASS: Yeah. The music.

BILLY: Be serious.

CASS: I am. You owe me a pint.

BILLY: The music don't count.

CASS: I got witnesses.

MAL: The Milky Bars are on Billy.

BILLY: Switch off, comedian.

MAL: What's wrong with Samson's?

BILLY: All right then! Samson's, Samson's! I said, I don't care! It's up to you! All right?

ALL: (*Sing:*) Billy's got the hump
    Billy's got the hump
    Ee aye addio
    Billy's got the hump!

BILLY: I ent in the fucking mood, all right?

MAL: Language.

BILLY: I said . . . !

CASS: All right, boys. Samson's it is.

BILLY: Right then. Good. Samson's it is. (Fucking dive . . .)

CASS: (*Aside to* BILLY) What's the matter?

BILLY: It's me birthday.

CASS: Shit. I fucking forgot.

BILLY: No, it ent that. It's just . . . I'm twenty. Cass . . . twenty years!

CASS: So?

BILLY: So a man is past his sexual peak, you know?

CASS: Is that a fact?

BILLY: Uh–hu.

CASS: Tch. Ent life a bitch.

KENNO: Samson's?

BILLY: Yeah. (Piss-hole . . .)

KENNO: I'm barred.

BILLY: Yeah?

KENNO: Yeah.

BILLY: When was this?

KENNO: Friday last.

BILLY: What did I tell you? Bunch of shitheads. What happened?

KENNO: I got pissed.

BILLY: Well, what do they expect? It's a pub, innit?

KENNO: I went through some plate glass.

BILLY: Big fucking deal. Friday night? What's their profit Friday night?

MAL: It's staggering.

BILLY: Exactly. We go in there, what are we drinking? Champagne. And why?

KENNO: Cos that's the one thing they can't water down.

BILLY: I ask you. No fucking scruples, some people. What are their priorities? I mean I'm not a commie but fucking hell. We go there tonight, we smash two windows.
(*Disco music. The scene is now a disco pub.* HARRY *wears a tuxedo and bow tie.*)

CASS: Bottle of champagne and a packet of crisps, please. Prawn cocktail flavour.

HARRY: Evening, boys.

KENNO: Hello, Harry. How's business?

HARRY: Business is booming. Hello, Terry.

TERRY: Hello, Harry.

BILLY: (*To the audience*) Harry Kellerway was a bouncer. One of Millwall's oldest thugs. He didn't have to work. He just enjoyed the aggravation.

HARRY: I want you to pay me what you owe me.

TERRY: Can we talk about this?

HARRY: No.

TERRY: Harry. We got a relationship.

HARRY: Listen, you young cunt. You pay me tomorrow or I break a fucking bottle in your head. Now look in my eyes and tell me I'm joking. (*Pause.*) Everything all right, boys? Behave yourselves, won't you.

(HARRY *goes.*)

TERRY: Jesus.

CASS: Here are, son. Drink this. What's the problem?

TERRY: It's nothing. I can handle it. It's just his attitude fucks me off.

BILLY: (*To the audience*) Kellerway used to piss on people. That was his trademark.

CASS: How much you owe him?

TERRY: Nah. I just got to move some shirts.

BILLY: (*To the audience*) One time we was up at Derby. There was fucking murders. This copper is in the car park, giving some geezer the kiss of life. Kellerway goes over, gets out his dick, pisses on the copper's back. He was a right fucking dog.

(THE LADS *are sizing up the talent.*)

KENNO: State of that.

MAL: Where? Where?

KENNO: The red shoes.

MAL: The yellow jumpsuit?

KENNO: Bag over the head job, that.

MAL: You think so?

KENNO: Two out of ten is generous.

MAL: I don't know. She's a nice dancer. Looks ent everything.

12

KENNO: Hello hello. Malcolm's turning queer.

MAL: Oh fuck off.

KENNO: She's built like a weightlifter. Look at them shoulders.

MAL: She's got a nice smile.

KENNO: You go for the dominating type, do you? Traffic wardens in rubber corsets, that kind of thing.

MAL: She's got a nice personality.

KENNO: And suspender belts and them little black lacy . . .

MAL: And she's intelligent.

KENNO: How can you tell that?

MAL: I used to go out with her.

KENNO: Yeah?

MAL: Yes.

(*Pause.*)

KENNO: What's her name?

MAL: Fatima.

KENNO: Nice name. (*Pause.*) Oh my God. Oh my GOD!

MAL: Where? Where?

KENNO: Tell me it's not true. Tell me I'm dreaming.

MAL: Where, Kenno?

KENNO: What is that woman wearing? That is disgusting. That is obscene. I think I'm in love. I want to cry.

MAL: Jesus. She might of come here on a bus. Think about that.

KENNO: She's probably got a coat, Malcolm.

MAL: I would certainly hope so. There's some funny people about.

KENNO: I've caught her eye.

MAL: Yeah?

KENNO: I've caught her eye.

MAL: I think you have.

KENNO: She's coming over here.

MAL: OK.

KENNO: Relax.

MAL: OK.

KENNO: Smile.

(THE LADS *watch as the woman walks past.*)

I hate these bitches they KNOW – you know? – they KNOW. That type really fucks me off. Fucking dykes. You want to get laid, ignore the bitches.

BILLY: Remember Beverley?

CASS: Beverley who?

BILLY: Beverley used to knock about with Kenno.

CASS: The name rings a bell.

BILLY: Legs up to her arse.

CASS: That Beverley.

BILLY: Yeah.

CASS: She was fit, man.

BILLY: She's let herself go.

CASS: You seen her?

BILLY: Yeah.

CASS: What's she doing these days?

BILLY: Pushing a pram.

CASS: Well. I'm not surprised.

BILLY: She was.

CASS: Them chicks, they leave school: sixteen years old, all they want is have a baby.

BILLY: (*To the audience*) There was a case the other day. Young mother, nineteen. She's only pushing a pram across the Old Kent Road, ent she, the dozy bitch. Up near the Elephant, this was. Thick with traffic and there she is, dodging about between the bumpers with a pram. I ask you. There's a kiddie in that pram. There's a pedestrian crossing five yards away. And she's stood there on the white lines, pram stuck out in front of her, in the fast lane. About as clever as a cow on a railway track. Anything could happen. The roads are packed with maniacs. Bus drivers cut you up left, right and centre. Messenger boys weaving about like Torvill and Dean. I tell you, that woman . . . people like her, they should not be allowed to have kids, and that is all there is to it. They should be sterilized. I promise you.

(MARIO *sings to himself. The scene is now the caff.* BILLY *and* CASS *arrive.*)

MARIO: Hallo, boys. What for you I do?

BILLY: Two sausage double egg bacon chips and a fried slice please Mario.

CASS: Twice.

MARIO: Two Great English Breakfast coming up. DUE
SALSICCIE UOVO PANCETTA PATTATINE FRITTE E LA
PANE FRITTO!

COOK: (*Off*) Pronto!

(BILLY *and* CASS *sit down.* BILLY *reads a paper.*)

BILLY: Can you believe this shit?

CASS: What?

BILLY: This is such shit. (*Pause.*) Oh no. Oh no. Oh no. This is
too much. I mean for fuck sake who reads this bollocks?
They need their head tested.

CASS: What?

BILLY: Listen to this. Listen to this. (*Pause.*) Oh that is out of
hand that is. I can't believe that. They got a fucking nerve
printing that.

CASS: What?

BILLY: Here are. Here are.

(*Pause.*)

CASS: Yeah?

BILLY: That's it. I refuse to go on reading this, this . . .

CASS: Let's have a look.

BILLY: Get off. Buy your own.

(TERRY *arrives. He has been beaten up.*)

TERRY: Cup of tea, please.

MARIO: I don't want no trouble.

TERRY: Two sugars.

MARIO: Sugar on the table. No trouble, OK?

BILLY: What happened, Terry?

CASS: Sit down here. Mario, get some ice.

TERRY: How does my nose look? Is it broke?

CASS: I don't think so. How does it feel?

TERRY: It hurts when I breathe.

CASS: Breathe through your mouth.

TERRY: That's what I'm doing. Sometimes I forget.

BILLY: Who did this?

TERRY: I can't tell you that.

CASS: It was Kellerway.

TERRY: It might of been, yes. I'm not saying anything.

CASS: I'll kill him.

TERRY: Listen. I deserved this. I fucked up.

CASS: Don't talk shit. You're half his size.

TERRY: I fucked up, Cass. I had a debt to pay.

BILLY: How much?

TERRY: Well. I was short of a ching.

BILLY: Five quid?

TERRY: It was the principle of the matter.

BILLY: You mug.

TERRY: Listen. Don't get involved.

CASS: Terry . . .

BILLY: I got no time for this fuckhead.

MARIO: Hey, boys. Shutup you mouth.

CASS: Sorry, Mario.

MARIO: Please. Cut the fucks. I got other customers. I like you but you bad for business.

BILLY: Sorry, Mario.

MARIO: That's OK. I don't want no trouble.

CASS: Listen, Terry . . .

BILLY: Listen. Cass is gonna tell you something.

CASS: I'm disappointed, Terry. I don't know what to think.

TERRY: What?

CASS: Friendship is a thing, Terry.

TERRY: Uh–hu.

CASS: Don't tell me don't get involved. It hurts me you say that. It offends me. It insults me.

TERRY: I'm sorry, Cass.

CASS: You have put a doubt in my mind. I don't know what you're thinking. Maybe you're thinking I'm a nonce.

TERRY: No . . .

CASS: I don't know.

TERRY: (Oh shit.)

BILLY: You should of come to us, Terry. We help each other out, we back each other up. That's what your mates are for.

TERRY: I was frightened.

BILLY: What was you frightened of?

TERRY: I don't know. Everything.

CASS: Come on, Terry. Spit it out.

(*Pause.*)

16

TERRY: I swear to God (oh shit) . . . I had a habit, a little habit but I swear to God I'm finished with it now, you got to believe me, I've learnt my lesson, I know I been dumb, I'm sorry, Cass, I'm sorry . . .

BILLY: Empty your pockets.

TERRY: What?

BILLY: Empty your pockets.

TERRY: What for?

BILLY: Just do it.

TERRY: Now?

BILLY: Yes.

   (TERRY *empties his pockets.*)
   What's this?

TERRY: Kitchen foil.

CASS: Oh Terry.

BILLY: 'What for'? I'll give you what for. You skag shit JUNKY!
   (BILLY *slaps* TERRY *hard across the face.*)

CASS: Billy. . . !

BILLY: The kid has got to learn, Cass.

TERRY: I'm sorry. I'm sorry.

CASS: You told a lie, Terry. You should of trusted us.

TERRY: I know.

CASS: OK.

BILLY: Cass: listen. I have to say this (and I don't mean this like it sounds):

CASS: What?

BILLY: He is a dead weight, a passenger and a liability to the firm. If I am any judge of character . . .

CASS: Save it, Billy.

BILLY: I know one when I see one.

TERRY: Cass. . . ?

CASS: What?

TERRY: Are you pissed off with me?

CASS: You shouldn't of told the lie.

TERRY: I should of known better.

CASS: Just remember in future.

TERRY: I promise.

CASS: OK.

17

BILLY: Word gets round, Cass. We'll be a laughing stock. 'Millwall is harbouring junkies.' Face it: once an addict, always an addict. You cannot break the same egg twice. Terry is a egg.

TERRY: Cass. . . ?

CASS: What?

TERRY: Are you still pissed off with me?

CASS: No. I don't think so.

BILLY: Who's been selling you this shit?

(*Pause.*)

TERRY: I can't tell you that.

(BILLY *and* CASS *burst into the disco pub.* BILLY *has a baseball bat in an Adidas bag. They accost* HARRY.)

BILLY: KELLERWAY! ON THE FLOOR, YOU SCUM! ON THE FLOOR! YOU FUCKING PIMP!

CASS: Listen to me, Harry: let's be reasonable: if I hear you making any more threats, I'll kill you then I'll fuck your wife. Is that understood?

HARRY: You nigger shit.

CASS: Let's keep politics out of this, Harry. You understand me. This is your language I'm talking. I don't like it but you force my hand. Your business is filth. You poison my friends. I'm warning you: don't fuck about with decent people. Don't make that mistake. Let's chip.

(*They dump the shirts on* HARRY *and go.*)

BILLY: (*To the audience*) That is how you keep the peace. You have to give it to 'em strong. Otherwise people take liberties: it's only human nature.

(*The scene is now a gym.* CASS *is working out.* TERRY *watches.* BILLY *reads a paper,* MAL *and* KENNO *with him.*)

TERRY: You don't mind me watching?

CASS: No.

TERRY: It don't put you off?

CASS: No.

TERRY: You sure?

CASS: Yes.

MAL: Come on, Cass. Ent you had enough? I'm working up a thirst just sitting here.

KENNO: (*Aside to* MAL) All that effort and no fucking dividend.
     I can't see the point meself.
MAL: (*Aside to* KENNO) Well, you want to represent your
     country, you got to come from Brixton these days, ent you?
BILLY: That's out of hand, Malcolm.
MAL: ('*Frank Bruno*') . . . know what I mean, Harry?
BILLY: Cut it out! All right?
MAL: Honestly. No sense of humour, some people.
BILLY: You should be on television, Mal. Then I could switch
     you off.
CASS: What's the matter?
BILLY: Nothing.
MAL: Come on. Let's go. I'm choking in here.
KENNO: You coming, Billy?
BILLY: I'll catch you up.
     (MAL *and* KENNO *go*.)
     Fucking joker . . .
CASS: You got to learn self-respect, Terry. People want to piss
     on you, no need to give 'em extra help. Listen: everyone
     is got a gift. Some people it's brains. Some people it's
     strength.
BILLY: (Some people it's both.)
CASS: Some people it ent so obvious. Most people, as it
     happens. But you was put here for a reason, Terry . . .
BILLY: (Believe it or not.)
CASS: All we got to do, we got to find out the reason.
BILLY: Life is short, Cass.
CASS: (*To* TERRY) Pay no attention. You want to give me a
     hand?
TERRY: I don't know what to do.
CASS: I'll show you.
TERRY: OK.
CASS: Right. Stand here.
TERRY: Here?
CASS: Yes.
TERRY: Now what?
CASS: We're doing bench presses.
TERRY: Bench presses.

CASS: Right. All you got to do, just put one finger under the bar when I'm failing.

TERRY: That's all?

CASS: Yes.

TERRY: One finger?

CASS: Yes.

TERRY: Which one?

CASS: Any one.

TERRY: It don't matter, right?

CASS: Right.

TERRY: Fuck, I could get into this.

CASS: Point being, I'm under pressure, I'm failing. One finger, this skims a few ounces off the top. We cheat the weight, I manage a couple, three more presses. The main thing is to keep going. This is what builds your power.

TERRY: Power, right.

CASS: Are you ready?

TERRY: Wait.

CASS: What?

TERRY: Can I ask a question?

CASS: What?

TERRY: How will I know when you're failing?

CASS: You'll know.

TERRY: How will I know?

CASS: (Jesus.)

TERRY: I'm sorry.

CASS: It's OK. Listen. I'll say something.

TERRY: Right. What will you say? For sake of argument.

CASS: I'll say 'now'.

TERRY: 'Now'.

CASS: Yes.

TERRY: OK. Let's go, let's go.

(CASS *starts*. TERRY *counts*. *Until* . . .)

CASS: Now.

TERRY: Now?

CASS: Yeah.

TERRY: Like this?

CASS: Yeah.

TERRY: Is this OK?

CASS: Yeah.

TERRY: Come on, Cass. Give it the big one.

CASS: (*Thrown*) What?

TERRY: 'Give it the big one'?

CASS: (*Relaxing*) Shit.

TERRY: Sorry, Cass. I was psyching you up.

CASS: I know. It just puts me off.

TERRY: Sorry.

CASS: That's all right.

TERRY: I'll learn.

CASS: You did OK.

TERRY: Yeah?

CASS: Sure.

TERRY: Thanks.

BILLY: Can we go now?

CASS: (*To* TERRY) You want to know my secret?

TERRY: Yeah.

CASS: Sport is played in the mind.

BILLY: See? Brains and beauty.

TERRY: Sport is played in the mind.

CASS: Yeah . . .

TERRY: Is that it?

CASS: What?

TERRY: The secret.

CASS: Everyone knows that. It's common knowledge.

TERRY: Oh.

CASS: This is the secret. The next thing I'm going to say is the secret, OK?

TERRY: Uh–hu.

CASS: All I do, I just say to meself: Right: twenty bench presses (whatever the fuck) or something will happen to my mum.

TERRY: Your mum.

CASS: Yeah.

TERRY: What?

CASS: Something (I dunno) fucking terrible. Like she falls down the stairs. She gets mugged. That kind of thing. See?

TERRY: Yeah.

CASS: And it is going to happen, this fucking terrible event, if I don't make the twenty. See?

TERRY: Is it?

CASS: I *believe* that, Terry.

TERRY: Uh–hu.

CASS: So I make the twenty. The next step, I go: right: five more or she's gonna get (and God forbid) like some incurable fucking . . .

TERRY: . . . right . . .

CASS: . . . disease, right. I mean, touch wood . . .

TERRY: Touch wood, yeah.

CASS: But once you have started on that train of thinking . . .

TERRY: . . . right, you can't . . .

CASS: . . . you can't stop.

TERRY: Exactly.

CASS: Which is the whole fucking psychology.

TERRY: Behind it.

CASS: Yes.

BILLY: (My my, is that the time?)

CASS: Because if you are serious in your heart . . . and you really *are* . . . then you will move mountains and uproot fucking trees . . .

TERRY: . . . right . . .

CASS: . . . if that is what it takes, am I right?

TERRY: Yes.

CASS: Course I am.

BILLY: Amen.

(*Sunday. A Catholic church.* BILLY *and* CASS *sit on a pew.*)

PRIEST: (*Off*) The Lord be with you.

RESPONSE: And also with you.

PRIEST: A reading from the Holy Gospel according to Matthew.

RESPONSE: Glory to you, Lord.

PRIEST: 'I say unto you, Love your enemies, bless them that curse you, do good to them that hate you, and pray for them which despitefully use you, and persecute you;

'That ye may be the children of your Father which is in heaven: for he maketh his sun to rise on the evil and on the good, and sendeth rain on the just and on the unjust.' This

22

is the gospel of the Lord.

RESPONSE: Praise to you, Lord Jesus Christ.

PRIEST: The peace of the Lord be with you always.

RESPONSE: And also with you.

PRIEST: Let us offer each other the sign of peace.

(BILLY *and* CASS *shake hands and murmur* Peace be with you *to people around them and finally to each other.*

Saturday. A street. CASS, BILLY *and* TERRY *come from one way,* KENNO *and* MAL *from the other.* KENNO *has a ghetto blaster.*)

KENNO: All right?

CASS: (*Does some body-popping moves.*) Well cheered up.

BILLY: Any sign of their mob?

MAL: Not yet.

BILLY: Where's the Bill?

MAL: New Cross Gate. They got a big escort.

BILLY: They'll need it today.

TERRY: I got to have a piss.

CASS: You just went.

TERRY: I got to go again.

KENNO: You nervous?

TERRY: Course not. A bit.

BILLY: Just be calm. Don't panic. Any trouble, stand your ground.

TERRY: Right.

BILLY: Stand your ground, that's the main thing. Don't panic. Be calm.

TERRY: Right.

BILLY: That's the main thing. Where's the Bill?

MAL: New Cross Gate.

BILLY: Is it cold or is it just me?

MAL: You got your jumper on inside out.

BILLY: Anyone got any chewing gum?

(*A* MOUNTED POLICEMAN *comes on.*)

MOUNTED POLICEMAN: All right, you lads. Break it up, come on. Move along.

BILLY: See you inside.

(*They split up. The scene is now the Den. The Coldblow*

Lane end.)

KENNO: Come on you Lions! Wake up! Christ. What they give 'em at half-time? Bournvita?

MAL: This is wank. How unusual, I must say.

BILLY: (*To the audience*) True, it was the Third Division. But, thing is, Third, Fourth Division, the defences are weak, right? So the football, right, is bang on. Plenty of chances, plenty of attack . . .

MAL: Chop him!

BILLY: . . . and a fair bit of that and all. Course, nine times out of ten we was on the wrong end of a big score, but still: what was Millwall famous for?

(*They do the Vikings chant:* The Lions . . . War! *Followed by the Millwall Nutty War Dance.*)

It was just the fans. Best fans in the country, Millwall. When the name of the game was chinning people, we was second to none. Well, you got to be best at something, ent you.

MAL: You skiving northern bastards! Get yourself a fucking job!

BILLY: (*To the audience*) You almost felt sorry for the opposition. They'd of got a warmer welcome on the moon.

THE LADS: (*Sing:*)
> Sign on, sign on
> With hope in your heart
> And you'll never get a job
> You'll never get a job.

(*They wave £10 and £20 notes and jeer.*)

KENNO: Bet you never seen one of these before!

MAL: On your bike, you lazy gits!

(*The* GOALKEEPER *crouches.*)

CASS: Man on! Man on! You dozy pricks!

TERRY: Chop him! Chop him!

(*Shrill blast of ref's whistle.*)

KENNO: Rubbish, ref! That was outside the area!

MAL: He took a dive!

KENNO: YOU BLIND CUNT! HE TOOK A DIVE!

(*They chant* Cheat Cheat Cheat *until there is another blast on the whistle.*)

24

CASS: I can't watch.
    (*The penalty is taken. The* KEEPER *goes the wrong way. A roar from the other end, followed by singing of:* You're supposed to win at home, *and* You're not singing any more. *As* THE LADS *move off, they sing:* We'll see you all outside.)
TERRY: The match ent finished yet.
BILLY: What's that got to do with it?
    (*Outside the ground they hang about. Distant cheering and singing.*)
POLICEMAN: What you lads waiting for? Come on, shift yourselves. Stop. You are not going that way, you are going this way. Now move! Oi! You! Come back here. What's the score?
KENNO: Three–nil to them.
POLICEMAN: Tch. All right. On your way now. Nice and orderly. (Three–nil. Tch.)
BILLY: Where do they change?
MAL: Whitechapel for King's Cross.
BILLY: Split up. We'll see you there. You go by car.
    (*The scene is now the Underground. The corridor echoes.* THE LADS *are running, singing:* We are Millwall, super Millwall and South London, LA LA LA. A NORTHERNER *runs at them.*)
NORTHERNER: All fucking mouth, you cockney shite!
CASS: Look out, he's got a knife!
NORTHERNER: Eh lads: leave the nigger to me. I'll give him a dig.
BILLY: (*Produces knife.*) I'll unzip your bollocks first, you . . . COME HERE!
    (Scuffle.)
CASS: FILTH! FILTH!
BILLY: Where?
CASS: GO GO GO!
    (ALL *scatter.*)
BILLY: (*To the audience*) You don't have time to think. Cos if you think, you're fucked. It's all reflex. Fear is an invitation. Sod's law: the knife is looking for the man who is looking for the knife. Believe me. My worst fear was

getting peeled. But when it happened, I didn't even notice. All you feel, you feel like a thump. I was wearing this shirt and there's a bit of a breeze and the shirt starts flapping and I put me hand there to tuck it in and that's when I knew. Because it was warm and wringing wet. I must of lost a pint. I thought I was gonna die.

But you can't let a little thing like that put you off. In fact I reckon I got even nuttier. Yeah. I just felt lucky.

(THE LADS *going home.*)

KENNO: We run 'em! We run 'em! We fucking run the mugs!

MAL: They was away on their toes. It was a walkover.

KENNO: They was some right hard cunts and all.

MAL: Hard? They was evil. And scruffy. Even their faces was scruffy.

KENNO: But we run 'em!

MAL: Yeah.

KENNO: We went through 'em like shit through a goose.

MAL: Yeah.

KENNO: Let's get drunk. Let's find some women. I'm well cheered up. Like a bull in season. Gentlemen, we have done our duty. We have had a right good day.

CASS: What's the matter, Billy?

(BILLY *takes off his shirt: it's covered in blood.*)

BILLY: Blood. (Fuck.)

(*He passes out.*

BILLY, KENNO *and* MAL *play cards.* CASS *reads a paper.* TERRY *sits.*)

CASS: (*Reads:*) 'If we are ever unlucky enough to have Millwall here again we shall put them in an enclosure and ask Whipsnade Zoo about the best way to control these animals.'

BILLY: 'Animals'?

CASS: That's what it says.

BILLY: What do they mean, 'animals'?

CASS: I don't know.

BILLY: We're all animals.

CASS: I know.

BILLY: A human being is an animal.

CASS: I know.

KENNO: Concentrate on the game.

BILLY: What do they mean, 'animals'?

CASS: I don't know.

BILLY: They put us in cages, what do they expect? (Raise you.) You can't be proud of nothing these days. It's just a dirty word.

KENNO: That's your five. That's my five.

MAL: Fold.

BILLY: Raise you.

KENNO: See you for twenty.

BILLY: Pair of aces.

KENNO: Full house, nines and fives.

BILLY: Shit.

KENNO: That's life.

BILLY: Three nines?

KENNO: Uh–hu.

BILLY: I just put two back.

KENNO: When?

BILLY: Just now. Two nines.

KENNO: What are you saying? Are you accusing me of something here?

BILLY: Did you shuffle the pack?

KENNO: No.

BILLY: (To MAL) Did he shuffle the pack?

MAL: No.

BILLY: I had two nines.

MAL: You must of made a mistake.

BILLY: I don't make mistakes at the card table!

KENNO: Come on, Billy. Learn to lose.

BILLY: I don't make mistakes.

KENNO: Then what am I? A cheat? Do I cheat you? Is that what you're saying?

BILLY: No . . .

KENNO: Check the pack.

BILLY: No . . .

KENNO: The cards are on the table. I put my hands up in the air. Check the pack.

BILLY: No . . . (Shit, what am I thinking?) Kenno, I'm sorry. I'm in a funny mood today, I don't know. Bobby's coming home. Everything.

KENNO: OK, OK. (You can't enjoy a decent game of poker with your friends . . .)

BILLY: Are you going?

KENNO: Yes. This game has lost its appeal quite frankly.

BILLY: You can't go.

KENNO: Where does it say I can't go?

BILLY: You just cleaned me out.

KENNO: Someone has to lose, Billy. It's a game.

BILLY: You reckon?

KENNO: Oh grow up.

BILLY: Yeah well fuck you.

KENNO: Fuck yourself.

BILLY: Come back here.

KENNO: What?

BILLY: Fuck off.

KENNO: I was just leaving, as it happens.

BILLY: And one more thing.

KENNO: What?

BILLY: I withdraw my apology.

KENNO: Anything else?

BILLY: No.

KENNO: See you Saturday.

BILLY: Twelve o'clock. Don't forget the carnations.

KENNO: Two dozen white.

(KENNO *goes*.)

BILLY: Did he shuffle the pack? Don't answer that question. I don't want to know. Bobby's coming home. I'm not gonna spoil the atmosphere.

CASS: Here, Terry. Is that you?

TERRY: Where?

CASS: In this picture: look.

TERRY: It is and all.

MAL: Your mum better not see that. You'll get a right bollocking.

TERRY: Fuck it. I'm a star.

BILLY: (*To the audience*) Bobby was away for six months that time, six solid months. I got two letters from him, postcards really. One he said the food was for pigs. The other was all Julie this, Julie that, how his balls was aching for it, but the food was getting better. I don't know why he joined the Navy in the first place.

(*The scene is now Portsmouth station.* BOBBY *in the bar. With him, an older man.*)

OLDER MAN: Cheers.

BOBBY: Cheers. (*Pause.*) Thanks.

OLDER MAN: Don't mention it. It's just a thing with me, well, it's more than a thing, it's a principle. I see a boy in uniform, I stand him a pint, no questions asked. Your very good health.

BOBBY: Cheers.

OLDER MAN: You're doing a grand job.

BOBBY: Thanks. (*Pause.*) Must be an expensive principle, town like Portsmouth.

OLDER MAN: You'd be surprised, young man.

BOBBY: Yeah?

OLDER MAN: Oh yes. People are not what they used to be.

BOBBY: No?

OLDER MAN: I get abuse. I have been hit.

BOBBY: Really?

OLDER MAN: This is not unknown. I want to buy a man a drink I don't know him I'm a what? a crank, a nutcase, a pervert, a monster. (*Pause.*) This is what it's come to.

BOBBY: Mm.

OLDER MAN: There's nothing left.

BOBBY: Ah.

OLDER MAN: The world has gone mad. (*Pause.*) Am I?

BOBBY: What?

OLDER MAN: Those things.

(*Pause.*)

BOBBY: You bought me a drink.

OLDER MAN: Exactly. I bought you a drink. What does that make me? (*Pause.*) We can't make gestures any more, we're savage fucking animals crawling in the wilderness. (*Pause.*)

29

You pay your taxes. You do this, you do that. It's not enough. People still die. People are lonely. Millions of them. Are alone. Men and women. In their millions. (*Pause.*) I'm not drunk. I talk too much. I like to talk.

BOBBY: That's all right with me.

(*Pause.*)

OLDER MAN: I was in the Forces.

BOBBY: Yeah?

OLDER MAN: Oh yes. I did my National Service. Changi, this was.

BOBBY: Where's that?

OLDER MAN: Singapore.

BOBBY: Nice one.

OLDER MAN: Square bashing. Rifle drill. Kit inspection. The whole damn routine. Two years bored rotten. What a bloody waste of life. I had plans. By Christ, I had plans. (*Pause.*)

BOBBY: I'm getting married.

OLDER MAN: I'm glad to hear it. I wish you many happy years.

BOBBY: Thank you.

OLDER MAN: Cheers. (*Pause.*) One word of advice.

BOBBY: What's that?

OLDER MAN: Don't have children.

(*Pause.*)

BOBBY: It's a bit late for that.

OLDER MAN: I see. Well . . . don't make the same mistake twice.

(*The train to London is announced.*)

BOBBY: That's my train. I have to go.

OLDER MAN: It's been a pleasure.

BOBBY: Thanks for the drink.

OLDER MAN: My honour.

BOBBY: Goodbye.

(BOBBY *knocks on* BILLY's *door.*)

Oi! Let me in, you scrawny bastard!

BILLY: Piss off, you old scumbag!

BOBBY: How you doing, fish face?

BILLY: All right till you turned up.

BOBBY: You look like shit.

BILLY: It runs in the family.

BOBBY: Aye aye: let's have a bit of respect, shall we. I been doing work of national importance.

BILLY: Beating up Yankee Bootnecks.

BOBBY: Come here, I'll fucking chin you.

BILLY: Yeah?

BOBBY: Yeah.

BILLY: Come on then. Let's see what the Navy's taught you.

BOBBY: You want a demonstration, do you?

BILLY: Yeah. Go on. Come for me. Kill me dead.

BOBBY: (*'Clint Eastwood'*) Do you feel lucky? Huh? Punk? Do you feel lucky?

BILLY: (*'De Niro'*) You talking to me? Huh? You talking to me?

BOBBY: (*'Scum'*) Where's your tool?

BILLY: (*Ditto*) What fucking tool?

BOBBY: (*Ditto*) This fucking tool!

> (*They grapple.* BILLY *cries out in pain.*)

You all right, Billy?

BILLY: Yeah.

BOBBY: What's the matter with you?

BILLY: Nothing. I got done at football.

BOBBY: Let's have a look. You want to change this dressing.

> (*Throughout the following,* BOBBY *changes* BILLY's *dressing.*)

BILLY: I give as good as I got though. Don't you worry about that.

BOBBY: I bet you did.

BILLY: I wish you was there, Bobby. You would of been proud.

BOBBY: You are a silly boy.

BILLY: What?

BOBBY: Fighting over football teams.

BILLY: That's choice coming from you.

BOBBY: I suppose it is.

BILLY: We're a fighting family, the Jarvises. It's in the blood, innit? We have to fight.

BOBBY: No one has to fight.

BILLY: What am I gonna be called? A coward?

BOBBY: All right, Billy. Let's not . . .

BILLY: I won't take shit from a northerner, Bobby. You know me on this subject. Any northerner comes down here, walks through this manor, spitting on me, I'll soon sort him out.

BOBBY: Yeah yeah.

BILLY: It's self-defence. That's what it comes down to.

BOBBY: This fucking place, eh? Nothing changes, does it? Everything stays the same.

BILLY: Well, I'm sorry if we ent good enough for you. You want me to ring the Dorchester?

BOBBY: Calm down, Billy. I like it this way. It's home. Do I look different?

BILLY: You've grown a beard.

BOBBY: Apart from the beard.

BILLY: No.

BOBBY: Oh.

BILLY: It suits you.

BOBBY: Moustaches ent allowed. You have to grow the full set. So you don't look like an Army ponce. See this badge?

BILLY: Uh–hu.

BOBBY: Engineering Mechanician.

BILLY: Is that good?

BOBBY: I got me trade. Invest in the future.

BILLY: Don't know why you bother with all that bollocks. You should of went into business with me.

BOBBY: I know your business.

BILLY: There's only one kind of business, Bobby.

BOBBY: I do what I like doing.

BILLY: Fair enough.

BOBBY: I *feel* different.

BILLY: What?

BOBBY: I feel too big for this room.

BILLY: You been away a long time, Bobby.

BOBBY: Yeah.

BILLY: Welcome home.

BOBBY: Let's get the fuck out of here.

BILLY: Where?

BOBBY: Let's just go somewhere.

(*The countryside of Surrey.* BOBBY *is fishing.*)

BILLY: (*Returning*) I just seen a squirrel.

BOBBY: Sh.

BILLY: Sorry.

BOBBY: Nervous fish, your tench.

BILLY: Sorry.

BOBBY: That's all right. You took your time.

BILLY: Couldn't find it. All shrivelled up like a little walnut.

BOBBY: That's the cold does that.

BILLY: Any luck?

BOBBY: Not a nibble.

BILLY: Sorry . . .

BOBBY: Not your fault. Open that flask.

BILLY: What is it?

BOBBY: Rum. Warm your cockles.

(*Pause.*)

BILLY: So tell me.

BOBBY: What?

BILLY: How's the Navy been treating you?

BOBBY: I told you.

BILLY: Tell me again. I like to hear it.

BOBBY: You make me laugh, you do.

BILLY: Nothing ever happens here.

BOBBY: Something happens everywhere.

BILLY: It's all right for you to talk. You're well out of it.

BOBBY: Would you swap places with me, then?

BILLY: Like a fucking shot.

BOBBY: Like fuck you would.

BILLY: I would. I'm sick of this place.

BOBBY: What do you want? See the world?

BILLY: Yeah. Why not?

BOBBY: You got a fucking television, ent you? What else do you need?

(*Long pause.*)

BILLY: Different world out here. Plenty of time. We should of brought a tent. I hate going back.

BOBBY: I'm getting married tomorrow.

BILLY: It's all here, Bobby. What do you need? A knife. A rod. You could live to be a hundred. (*Deep breath.*) Smell that.

BOBBY: What?

BILLY: Pig shit.

BOBBY: (*Deep breath.*) Sweet.

BILLY: I remember that tree.

BOBBY: Mm.

BILLY: Dad used to bring us here. Ent changed much, has it?

BOBBY: Nope. Still no fucking fish. You want a go?

BILLY: All right. See if I can remember how.

(BILLY *casts the line.*)

There. Sweet. Just like bowling.

BOBBY: You never forget.

BILLY: Nope. (*Pause.*) Talk about the Navy again.

BOBBY: It's a good life, Billy. You got your mates, you got your
food, you got your work. And these mates, they are the best
mates a man could wish for. They are more than mates.
Because why? Because any other job, Billy, what is the
bottom line? The sack. Out on your ear, back on the rock
'n' roll. This job, Billy, the bottom line is you are going to
get pinged off the face of the earth. You see what I'm
talking? This is not money shit, this is not
standard-of-living shit, this is real shit. This is real work.
And there is precious little of that about. I've told you all
this.

BILLY: I like to hear it. I'm sick of talking about money and
fucking. That's all I ever hear. I listen to meself sometimes.
(*Pause.*)

BOBBY: You know what?

BILLY: What?

BOBBY: We always used to be rowing.

BILLY: Did we?

BOBBY: Yeah. When we was little. There's a bit of fishing line
near your foot.

BILLY: Where?

BOBBY: Near your foot. Pick it up. Little birds get all tangled in
it starve to death.

BILLY: What shall I do with it?

BOBBY: Give it here, useless.

BILLY: (Moany git.)

34

BOBBY: Don't you start.

BILLY: You ent changed, have you?

BOBBY: Nor have you.

> (*Pause. They laugh.*)
>
> You make me laugh you do.

BILLY: Piss off.

BOBBY: How's all the Millwall?

BILLY: Same old faces. You'll see 'em all tonight.

BOBBY: Kellerway still a regular?

BILLY: He never was. Wouldn't catch that bastard travelling away. He's just a nobody. All he is is hard.

BOBBY: There's no hard men, Billy. Believe me, there ent no such thing.

BILLY: You don't know Kellerway.

BOBBY: Oh yes I do. I know a thing or two about Harry Kellerway. For one thing he used to support West Ham.

BILLY: Did he?

BOBBY: I know that for a fact.

BILLY: How come?

BOBBY: I'll tell you.

The old man, he took me to Upton Park once, years ago. I must of been about ten. Maybe it was me birthday, I can't remember. Anyway, it was me first ever real live football match. West Ham versus Millwall. Pre-season friendly. And the old man was treating me.

We come out the tube and we was walking up the road to the ground. We was early and there's hardly no one about. And we go past this caff and these skins come out, only four of 'em and one's not much older than me. And they're walking behind us. I remember the old man grabbing me hand and pulling me closer, like. But he didn't say nothing. He just kept on walking. And these skins ask us are we Millwall. Well, they didn't need to ask. I'm wearing me colours. Brand new scarf . . . yeah, it was me birthday. I remember now.

So they ask us are we Millwall but the old man keeps his mouth shut and he's staring straight ahead. And even when they stop us he keeps looking in front of him, looking right through them as if they weren't there. And he don't make a sound neither, not even when they've got him on the pavement and they're . . .

All I could think of was Mum'll go mad when she sees the state of that overcoat. He only had the one. And there it was getting covered in dog shit.

Anyway, it brought on one of his asthma attacks. So they all stood back and there he was, heaving on the pavement like a fish out of water. And then they pushed the little one forward, the youngest. Not much older than me, he was. And they told him to . . . wet on the old man. And he did.

Then they left us alone. They never touched me.

And after they was gone I just waited till the old man managed to catch his breath. Must of been a full five minutes. And then he got up and he sez come on and he grabs me hand. And we saw the match, but all I remember is wanting to tell him to wipe the blood off his mouth. But I didn't. And he never said a word, not then or ever. It was like it never happened. Except for the blood on his mouth and the piss and the shit on his coat.

Well, I'll tell you one thing. We had the carriage to ourselves on the train home.

And I'll tell you something else. That little skin, the youngest one, the one not much older than me. That was Kellerway. No mistake. That was Harry Kellerway.

(*The scene is now the disco pub.* BOBBY's *stag night.* THE LADS *lift* BOBBY *shoulder high and sing* 'For he's a jolly good fellow'. HARRY *comes over.*)

HARRY: Well well well. If it ent Bobby Jarvis I'm a monkey's uncle. We are honoured. What you drinking?

BOBBY: I'm all right.

HARRY: Cigar?

BOBBY: You want to give that up, Harry. You'll get cancer.

BILLY: You nonce.

BOBBY: Billy.

BILLY: Where was you last Saturday?

BOBBY: Billy.

HARRY: Now let me see. Last Saturday . . .

36

BILLY: We was at Brentford. Where was you?

HARRY: Up White Hart Lane, as it happens.

BILLY: Changed your religion, have you?

HARRY: Helping the yids kick fuck out the scallies.

BOBBY: Nothing changes, does it, Harry?

BILLY: Couldn't follow Millwall to Brentford. What kind of support is that?

BOBBY: Some people.

HARRY: Some people what?

BOBBY: Never grow up.

HARRY: You having a pop at me?

BOBBY: Don't get excited, Harry. I'll tell your probation officer.

HARRY: I can't hear what you're saying, Jarvis. Your mouth is full of shit.

BOBBY: Ignore him. He might go away.

HARRY: I hear congratulations are in order, Bobby.

BOBBY: What for? I ent done nothing.

HARRY: Don't be shy. You're getting married.

BOBBY: What's that to you?

HARRY: Nice girl, that Julie. Mind you, I couldn't do it to a cow like that.

BOBBY: You couldn't do it to your fist, Kellerway.

HARRY: I wouldn't need to, sailor boy.

BOBBY: (This cunt is annoying me.)

HARRY: We used to have a name for her. 'Martini'. 'Anytime, anyplace, anywhere . . .'

BOBBY: (*Advancing*) KELLERWAY!

(*They fight. As they fight,* BOBBY *talks.*)

What am I doing? . . . I'm too old for this really . . . I don't do this sort of thing no more . . . Julie don't like me rucking . . .

HARRY: You're under the thumb, mate.

BOBBY: I'm getting married tomorrow.

(*He KOs* HARRY.)

Christ, that felt good. I been wanting to do that for years. It's very . . . what's the word?

BILLY: Pleasant.

BOBBY: Nah nah.

37

BILLY: Pleasurable.

BOBBY: Therapeutic. Yeah. Like having a damn good crap. I mean you straighten your arm and it's like years of silt come dredging up from the bottom of your gut. Know what I mean?

BILLY: That's one way of putting it, yeah.

BOBBY: Don't half make your hand sting, though.

THE LADS: (*Sing:*)

> Nice one, Bobby
> Nice one, son
> Nice one, Bobby
> Let's have another one.

BILLY: (*To the audience*) It was the European Cup Final, Aston Villa versus Real Madrid. I was watching it on the box. I don't know what Villa thought they was playing but it certainly wasn't football. Sure they had most possession but the dagos had all the chances, didn't they? And there's Peter Withe poncing about like Rudolf Nureyev. Trying to do all that fancy Continental stuff, you know: no aggression, no attack.

Anyway, he scored. Yeah. Withe scored. Pure fluke, of course. But it was the match winner. And it was that goal what started it off. I was sitting in front of the box and I just froze. I couldn't believe my ears. It was the Madrid fans (them dago bastards) chanting 'Argentina Argentina'. I had a can of lager in me fist going warm and I crushed it. That was all I could do. Mum was out, thank Christ. She would of had a fit. The beer went everywhere.

FIRST SPEAKER: (*The House of Commons, 3 April 1982*) The House meets this Saturday to respond to a situation of great gravity. We are here because, for the first time for many years, British sovereign territory has been invaded by a foreign power. The government must now prove by deeds to ensure that foul and brutal aggression does not succeed in our world . . .

BILLY: (*To the audience*) And when the Villa fans started singing 'Rule, Britannia' I could feel the hairs standing up on me cobblers, I was that proud.

SECOND SPEAKER: The very thought that our people, one thousand eight hundred people of British blood and bone, could be left in the hands of such criminals is enough to make any normal Englishman's blood boil – and the blood of Scotsmen and Welshmen boil too.

BILLY: (*To the audience*) I never thought in a million years I'd have warm feelings for Aston Villa fans. But I did that night.

THIRD SPEAKER: We have lost a battle, but we have not lost the war. It is the old saying that Britain always wins the last battle. In the end in life it is self-reliance and only self-reliance that counts. The time for weasel words has ended.

BILLY: (*To the audience*) Oh yes, my friends. Cos we was all in the same boat, so to speak. Weren't we?

FOURTH SPEAKER: From next Monday, the Royal Navy will put to sea in wartime order and with wartime stock and weapons. That force will include the carriers HMS *Invincible* and HMS *Hermes*, the assault ship HMS *Fearless* . . .

BILLY: (*To the audience*) But what I don't understand is this. They still do it, don't they? The Spanish. The Germans. The French. The Italians. Whoever. If an English team is playing abroad, there's the rest of the world chanting 'Argentina Argentina'. I don't understand it, honest I don't. I mean, we won. Didn't we?
(*The Task Force. An assault ship.*)

RATINGS: (*Sing to the tune of 'Summer Holiday':*)
We're all going to the Malvinas
We're all gonna kill a spic or two
We're all going on a pusser's holiday
For a month or two
Or three or four.

We're gonna kill the wops with phosphorous
We'll get them with our GPMGs
They'd better not try to take cover
Cos there ain't no fucking trees.

BOBBY: Dear Billy. As I write to you the sun is shining and

glinting off the blades of a pristine Westland Sea King.

I feel very proud of my work. We all do. The atmosphere is very good, in fact. We had a right laugh crossing the Equator. Someone shaved my beard off. Was I on the telly? I think I might have been. There's cameras everywhere. It's a bit of a party really.

Billy. The reason I'm writing is this. I have got five tickets for Phase One of the World Cup. It is a package deal done by Sports Travel. Me and some mates bought them before *Indestructible* left Southampton. As we are now approaching . . .

BILLY: Censored.

BOBBY: . . . and you've probably seen on the news that . . .

BILLY: Censored.

BOBBY: . . . longer than I thought so, instead of getting a refund, I am sending the tickets to you.

BILLY: Bobby, you're a genius.

BOBBY: I know you will make good use of them. I wish I was coming with you. I hope you are looking after Julie like you said. Love . . .

BILLY: Bobby.

BOBBY: PS. Some of the lads have made out their will. I left you my fishing rod. It's a joke, isn't it?

CASS: Billy!

BILLY: What?

CASS: Need a flag, don't we? Cop hold of that end.
(*Between them they unfurl a Union Jack. Emblazoned across the middle are the words:* LEWISHAM NATIONAL FRONT.)
I had it off some Front lads.

BILLY: I thought they grew on trees.

CASS: They was on a march.

BILLY: How many?

CASS: Twenty, twenty-five.

BILLY: Is that all?

CASS: Plus the Bull.

BILLY: And you just steam in . . .

CASS: I just steam in, yes, that is correct, Brian. Arms and legs going like windmills. Took 'em completely by surprise.

BILLY: I expect you did.

CASS: What have I always said, Billy? Jump the bastards. You come screaming out of nowhere like a man on fire, you got the psychological advantage. Which is fucking exactly what I did, Billy.

BILLY: Yeah?

CASS: I reckon I got four seconds. Five at the outside. I case the situation. Fat geezer at the back. Suit and tie, Union Jack. I'll have him. It's shit or bust.

BILLY: Right.

CASS: I'm tingling, Billy. I'm like a sprinter in the blocks.

BILLY: Oh yes.

CASS: The rest is in slow motion. One . . . through the Bull, smell his aftershave . . . Two . . . jack the bastard in the kidneys . . . Three . . . cop the pole and swing it down – catches a cozzer one on the jaw.

BILLY: Sweet.

CASS: But I don't stop to ask if he's all right. I'm gone.

BILLY: Like a bullet.

CASS: Too right. I mean these chaps is well pissed off. They are breathing fire down my neck.

BILLY: Where is this?

CASS: Cowley Road.

BILLY: I'm with you.

CASS: I hang a left . . .

BILLY: . . . into the estate.

CASS: First block, first flight, first door, knock knock.
      – Let me in brother, the Bull is on my tail.
      – No way, man, there's kids in here.
      – And there's a piece in my jacket sez I'm the health visitor.

BILLY: Are you shitting me?

CASS: What's this look like? Scotch mist?

BILLY: Is this a wind up or what?

CASS: What you think, I made it meself?

BILLY: True.

CASS: Hang about.

BILLY: What?

CASS: Shit.

BILLY: What's wrong?

CASS: This Union Jack is back to front.

BILLY: That don't matter.

CASS: It ent correct.

BILLY: Still red white and blue, innit?

CASS: So's a bottle of Domestos but that don't make it a Union Jack.

BILLY: (*To the audience*) This was Cass. The philosopher.

    (BILLY *takes out a gun.*)

CASS: What's that?

BILLY: What's what?

CASS: That.

BILLY: This?

CASS: Yes.

BILLY: What is it?

CASS: Yes.

BILLY: What does it look like?

CASS: A gun.

BILLY: Then that's what it is. A thing is a thing, OK?

    (*Pause.*)

CASS: What are you doing?

BILLY: I'm taking it apart.

CASS: Why?

BILLY: It comes apart, see.

    (*Pause.*)

CASS: Where did you get it?

BILLY: A man.

CASS: Cost you?

BILLY: What do you think, you get coupons? (*Pause.*) I don't use it, I get my deposit back.

CASS: You don't need it.

BILLY: Don't start on that subject, please. Keep your fucking thoughts to yourself, OK?

CASS: What do you need it for? Give me one good reason.

BILLY: Self-defence.

CASS: Bollocks. A gun is asking for trouble, man.

BILLY: We're going to a foreign country. We don't have to ask

42

for trouble. We are in it. Up to our eyeballs.

CASS: You reckon?

BILLY: Fucking right I do.

CASS: That much?

BILLY: This much.

CASS: You're full of shit.

BILLY: Listen. I don't want to fall out over a silly little thing.
All I'm saying is, there are maniacs walking the streets,
every country in the world. This is a fact of life. All I'm
doing, squaring up to the fact, the English are sitting ducks
for any Tom Dick Hasta la Vista wants to prove he's king
of the dunghill, comes at you with a fucking axe, fucking
meat cleaver, for fuck sake. Please God this doesn't happen.

But, let's face it, the Spanish are a fucking barbaric
people. You see their cops? Most bastard police force in
Europe, Spain. You see the artillery hanging off them
geezers? They got the right idea. Don't give the fuckers an
inch. You still look worried.

CASS: You got live bullets?

BILLY: That's how they come.

CASS: Shit.

BILLY: Don't get the wrong idea, Cass. I think you're labouring
under one massive fucking delusion here. We don't *use* the
gun.

CASS: We don't?

BILLY: Shit, no.
(*Pause.*)

CASS: What happens the geezer comes at you with the cleaver?

BILLY: We cross that bridge when we come to it.
(*Pause.*)

CASS: Then why have we got the gun?

BILLY: In case.
(*Pause.*)

CASS: But we're not using it?

BILLY: Course not. What do you take me for? Some kind of a
moron?

CASS: Then why are we taking it, we're not using it?

BILLY: Because we need it, Cass.

43

CASS: But we're not using it.

BILLY: No.

CASS: Then why do we need it?

(*Pause.*)

BILLY: Because it is every man's God-given right to preserve his life and stay in one piece any fucking method he can. (*Pause.*) OK? (*Pause.*) Are you happy now?

CASS: No.

BILLY: Look, listen. Cass. Take it. Go on. Have a go. See how it feels. Good, yeah? See what I mean? Don't point it at me, for fuck sake.

CASS: Is it loaded?

(*He pulls the trigger: the chamber is empty.*)

BILLY: You pulled the trigger. You pulled the trigger and you didn't know it was loaded or not. ARE YOU MAD? YOU COULD OF KILLED ME!

CASS: It wasn't loaded.

BILLY: YOU DIDN'T KNOW THAT! Jesus. These things are dangerous.

CASS: How do you reckon on getting it through Customs?

BILLY: I've thought of that . . .

CASS: . . . yeah? . . .

BILLY: . . . I don't know. One possibility . . .

CASS: . . . yeah? . . .

BILLY: . . . it comes apart, right?

CASS: . . . yeah . . .

BILLY: So everyone takes a bit.

(*Pause.*)

CASS: How do we get past the metal detectors?

BILLY: The metal detectors?

CASS: Yeah.

(*Pause.*)

BILLY: This is good. This is positive planning. (*Pause.*) 'How do we get past the metal detectors?' That's a good question.

CASS: What's the answer?

BILLY: Let me work this one out. (*Pause.*) I got it.

CASS: What?

BILLY: There are no metal detectors.

44

CASS: No?

BILLY: No.

CASS: How do you know?

BILLY: I'm guessing. It's one possibility.

CASS: What if there are?

BILLY: 'What if there are?'

CASS: Yes.

> (*Pause.*)

BILLY: What the fuck is this, a fucking police state all of a sudden? People hijack airliners, for fuck sake! They manage! We're only going on a poxy cross-Channel ferry. (*To the audience*) I've had the same dream every night for two weeks. I'm swimming in the sea towards Bobby. To my right is a ship, all bright with fire and a great hole in its side. And Bobby is facing me, treading water. He's got on a navy wool pullover, but no cap. And I can hear the sound of the sea. As I swim towards him he disappears. And I wake up.

> (*A ship of the Task Force.* BOBBY *below decks. Two* MARINES, *above, on deck, at the rail.*)

BOBBY: Her Majesty's Ship *Indestructible*. A Type 42 Destroyer. Length overall 412 feet. Depth 19 feet. Beam 47 feet. Tonnage 3,500. Billy. This is beauty.

FIRST MARINE: What time does the bar open?

SECOND MARINE: What fucking bar?

BOBBY: Two Rolls-Royce Olympus gas turbines. 56,000 horsepower.

FIRST MARINE: There was a bar on the *Canberra*.

SECOND MARINE: You know what? I keep thinking we're going north.

BOBBY: Proceeding due south. Average rate 28 knots.

FIRST MARINE: And a buffet.

> (*The alarm sounds.*)

TANNOY VOICE: Air Raid Warning Red. Repeat. Air Red. This is not a drill. Repeat. This is not a drill.

SECOND MARINE: Where's the fucking air cover? What are those fucking Crabs playing at?

TANNOY VOICE: Take cover. Take cover.

45

(*An explosion as air-to-sea missile scores a direct hit.*)

LONE VOICE: (*Sings:*)

> Come all you pretty fair maids
> A line to you I'll write:
> In ploughing of the ocean
> I take a great delight.
> Our land it fears no danger
> Nor danger does it know
> While we poor jolly sailor lads
> Plough on, the ocean through.

JOHN NOTT (DEFENCE MINISTER): One of our ships has been badly damaged and she is in difficulties. I can't give any further details at the moment – the news about her is still coming in. Clearly from what we know at the moment it is bad news and I should say that straight away.

(*The Jarvis council flat. There is a telephone.* CASS *stands at window looking out. Pause.*)

CASS: It's gonna rain.

BILLY: You reckon?

CASS: Yes.

BILLY: I think you're right.

CASS: I am looking at one fuck of a bunch of clouds. And I'm sweating like a pig.

BILLY: What's the time?

CASS: I just told you.

BILLY: I forgot.

CASS: You want to watch the news?

BILLY: No. Yes. I dunno. Every time I hear that theme tune me tummy does fucking gymnastics.

CASS: I know.

BILLY: Shit.

(*Pause.*)

CASS: You know what?

BILLY: What?

CASS: That theme music . . .

BILLY: . . . yeah?

CASS: . . . to the news . . .

BILLY: . . . yeah?

CASS: . . . every time that music is played . . .

BILLY: . . . yeah . . .

CASS: . . . the geezer what wrote it . . .

BILLY: . . . the composer . . .

CASS: . . . right . . . gets twenty-five quid.

BILLY: You're full of shit.

CASS: Straight up.

BILLY: Twenty-five?

CASS: It was in the paper.

BILLY: That is fucking criminal, that is. How does a person get on to a fiddle like that?

CASS: It makes you wonder, don't it?

(*The phone rings.* BILLY *picks it up.*)

BILLY: Yes? . . . TERRY! Fuck me . . . I just felt all the blood rush to me feet . . . no, we ent heard nothing yet . . . no, I don't think I could handle a curry, mate (Cass, are you hungry?) . . .

CASS: Nah.

BILLY: . . . thanks, Terry . . . I'll call later if . . . yeah, bye . . . (*Hangs up.*) Heart in the right place, that boy.

CASS: Thick as pig shit.

BILLY: Nobody's perfect. What's the time?

CASS: You want to try that number again?

BILLY: It'll be engaged. Worse than fucking British Rail, the Navy.

CASS: I'll give it a whirl, Shirl.

BILLY: Thanks, Cass.

(*There is a knock at the door.*)

Euston Station, this place. There's some cans in the fridge. (*He opens the door to a Royal Naval* PADRE.) Yes?

PADRE: Does a Mrs Jarvis live here?

BILLY: Who wants her?

PADRE: My name is Ian Mellor. I'm a chaplain with the Royal Navy. I've just come from Greenwich . . .

BILLY: She's asleep.

CASS: Who is it, Billy?

BILLY: No one.

47

PADRE: I must speak to her. I have some news . . . May I come in?

BILLY: I'm sorry, you'll have to come back another day.

PADRE: I really must . . .

BILLY: Didn't you hear? I told you to piss off out of it! I'll call the police!

PADRE: Please let me in. It's starting to rain.

CASS: Let him in, Billy.

(BILLY *does so*.)

PADRE: Thank you.

CASS: Mrs Jarvis is sleeping. She's not very well. She's pregnant.

PADRE: Who are you?

BILLY: I'm his brother.

PADRE: The brother of . . . Robert Anthony Jarvis?

BILLY: Yes, sir.

CASS: Anthony?

PADRE: I'm afraid it's bad.

BILLY: What is?

PADRE: The news, Mr Jarvis.

BILLY: I don't understand, sir.

PADRE: Your brother died at four o'clock yesterday morning. He was killed in action. I'm sorry.

(BILLY *strikes the* PADRE *across the face*.)

CASS: (*Intervening*) Billy, for fuck sake . . . I'm sorry . . .

PADRE: No, no. It's . . .

CASS: Are you all right?

PADRE: Yes.

BILLY: Would you like a cup of tea?

PADRE: Um . . .

BILLY: Or there's some beer if you prefer it.

PADRE: Tea would be fine.

BILLY: How did he die?

PADRE: There is a telephone number . . .

BILLY: I saw him three weeks ago. He was standing in this room.

PADRE: Yes.

BILLY: I don't understand this.

48

PADRE: I have a map which you may keep. Here. The 'X' marks the spot where he was buried at sea.

BILLY: I don't want him buried at sea.

PADRE: It's a Naval tradition.

BILLY: I want to see him. I'm his brother. I've got a right . . .

PADRE: A sailor has two families, Mr Jarvis. Each as caring as the other. Believe me. Robert is at peace.

BILLY: Did you know him?

PADRE: We never met.

(*Pause.*)

CASS: I'll make the tea.

(CASS *goes. Pause.*)

PADRE: Would you like to pray?

BILLY: Pardon?

PADRE: Shall we say a short prayer together?

BILLY: No, I can't. I'm sorry.

PADRE: Why not at least try? Prayer can be a true comfort in times of trouble. You don't have to believe.

BILLY: I go to church every week, Padre. We're Catholic. That's all.

PADRE: Oh. I'm sorry. I wasn't told.

BILLY: No.

(*Pause.*)

PADRE: Mr Jarvis . . . I know it comes as a great shock when a healthy young man dies in such an unexpected way, but I do think . . . you can be proud of your brother. He gave his life in the service of his country. You can be proud of how he died.

BILLY: I didn't need him to die to feel proud of him.

(*Long pause.*)

CASS: Milk and sugar?

PADRE: I have another call to make. There are others, Mr Jarvis.

BILLY: I don't care about the others.

PADRE: There is a telephone number. If there is anything you need . . . I have to mention . . . the matter of compensation. Mrs Jarvis will be notified by post in due course. And I must ask you . . . not to speak to the Press.

(*The* PADRE *goes.*)

BILLY: Where's my coat?

CASS: Where you going?

BILLY: For a walk. I need some air.

CASS: What about Julie?

BILLY: Julie? (*To the audience*) The war was over for her. She never bothered with the news after that. She just lay in a corner of their bed for a week. She lost two stone. She was smoking forty a day. We had to hide it from the doctor. The kid was early. Six pounds two ounces. But it was perfect. And it was a boy. They hadn't decided on a name.

CASS: Hang about. I'm coming with you.

(*They go out. The thunderstorm rages.*)

BILLY: (*To the audience*) I must of walked all over London that night. I remember standing on Blackfriars Bridge. And it was raining. And the rain was warm, as warm as blood.

CASS: Slow down, Billy. I can't keep up.

BILLY: What time is it?

CASS: One thirty, two. I've lost track. We should get back to Julie . . .

(BILLY *starts undressing.*)

What are you doing?

BILLY: It's all right, Cass. The rain is warm. That's how we know it's summer.

CASS: Come on, Billy. You'll catch a cold.

BILLY: Don't touch me!

CASS: All right, all right.

(BILLY *jumps on to the wall of the bridge.*)

Jesus Christ, be careful!

BILLY: Cass: look. What do you see?

CASS: Billy, come down. You're making me nervous.

BILLY: The docks, the bridges, the domes and the steeples. Cass . . .

CASS: Yes, Billy.

BILLY: This whole city is asleep.

CASS: I know.

BILLY: WAKE UP, YOU BASTARDS!

CASS: (Oh my God . . .)

50

BILLY: How can they sleep? They should be told.

CASS: No, Billy . . .

BILLY: You honest people! hard-working people! you people
who can sleep at night! There is damp in your cellars and
rats in your drains! Your children are not safe! For the
Lord thy God sendeth his rain to fall on the evil and on the
good, on the just and on the unjust, on the fat and on the
thin so YOU BETTER WATCH OUT! God farts. God pisses.
God shits on my head and gives me a spoon to eat it with. I
have fit myself for this disgrace. All my fucking life.
(*Pause*.)

CASS: Come down, Billy. Put your coat on.

(BILLY *does so*.)

BILLY: Cass . . !

CASS: What?

BILLY: What was the last thing I said to him?

CASS: To Bobby?

BILLY: I had a dream, Cass. I saw it happen. I knew, Cass! I
knew! I should of told him. I should of said something. I
should never of let him go!

CASS: Stop it, Billy! That is stupid. You know it is.

BILLY: Yeah. Yeah. You're right. I'm sorry . . .

CASS: Don't apologize. I don't care, do I? It's just grief, innit?
It's only natural. I feel it too, you know.

BILLY: Thank God you're here, Cass. I can talk to you. I think
I'd go mad with all these thoughts come crashing through
my head. My brain is on fast-forward. I see him burning
like a guy on a bonfire, curling up . . . I need hard
information, Cass. I don't want to go mad. Make sure I
don't. I'm being serious.

CASS: I know you are. Look at me. I'm with you, Billy. (*Pause*.)
Now let's go home.

BILLY: No.

CASS: This is not doing us any good.

BILLY: I don't want to go back there, not yet. Let's walk some
more.

CASS: All right then. If we're gonna walk, let's fucking walk.
(CASS *leads. They walk*.)

51

BILLY: Euston. Camden. Archway and back. Hyde Park.
Victoria. We stop on the Embankment.
(*They sit on a bench. Behind the bench is a war memorial,
marked 'Lest We Forget': a cluster of Tommies in heroic
posture: one points, one raises the standard, etc. A* TRAMP
approaches.)

TRAMP: (*Scots*) Give us 20p for a cup of tea.

BILLY: Piss off. You stink.

TRAMP: So would you if you were me.

CASS: (*Giving coin*) Here are, Jock.

TRAMP: Good luck to you, sir. Will ya no shake ma hand? I'm
an old soldier, ya ken.

BILLY: Which war did you fight in?

TRAMP: All of 'em. The lot. Every fucking one. Here. (*Displays
a medal.*) That's the Distinguished Service Order.

BILLY: Sell it and take a bath.

TRAMP: A medal is worth more than money, ya ken. I was
mentioned in despatches fifteen times. Will ya no shake ma
hand?
(CASS *does so.*)
Good luck to you, sir. You're a gent.
(*The* TRAMP *goes.* CASS *falls asleep.*)

BILLY: I couldn't sleep. I'll never sleep.
I dare not sleep, cos if I do
I'll dream of swallowing salt water
in a black and frozen ocean . . .
and there he sleeps, his eyes wide open,
floating like a pickled gherkin
beneath a solid mile of ice.
(*The* STATUES *speak as the* GHOST)

GHOST: Billy, Billy. Can you see me? Can you hear me?

BILLY: Fucking Ada.

GHOST: It's me. Your brother. Bobby Jarvis.
Mechanician. Lost at Sea.
(*Pause.*)
What's the matter? Ent you pleased to see me?

BILLY: No, it's just . . . I didn't recognize you without the
beard, that's all. Are you coming home, Bobby?

52

GHOST: I can hardly do that, can I?
BILLY: Why not?
GHOST: I woulda thought that was obvious. I'm dead, you
    pillock.
BILLY: What happened, Bobby?
GHOST: She sank like a coin
    in a swimming pool.
BILLY: Just give me a name
    and I promise you, brother,
    there ent a dark corner
    of this fucking planet
    where he can hide from me:
    I'll hunt like a foxhound
    and cling like a ferret,
    I'll run him to ground
    and he'll shit steaming bricks –
    to my fist he'll be mincemeat
    and pulp to my boot.
GHOST: That's my boy. I find you apt.
    But you ent had the full s.p.

    I serviced that sweetheart myself, I did –
    each moving part runs smooth as oil,
    the instruments wink merrily,
    for I am handy, artful, crafty.

    But Billy, all my skill is wasted –
    gone to waste, my strength, my pride:
    it was murder that day, murder:
    Johnny Gaucho caught us napping,
    diving from the clear blue sky.
    Aluminium, plastic lagging
    turned my ship into a prison:
    we met our doom in burning water:
    I tasted fire, I tasted sea salt,
    I heard the screams of my companions,
    cruel screams; and – in a dream –
    I heard my own voice screaming with them.

Burning oil stuck to my flesh
and melted me like polystyrene . . .

BILLY: NO!

GHOST: And so I died. I died the death.
The rest is . . . up to you.

BILLY: Bobby! BOBBY!

(*The* GHOST *is gone.*)

Cass! Wake up, wake up.

CASS: (*Wakes up, looks around.*) Shit.

(*Bright morning sunlight.*)

BILLY: (*To the audience*) I felt special that morning. Nine a.m.
we're in the West End. And I'm wide awake.

CASS: (*Yawns.*) I'm glad to hear it.

BILLY: The sun's on our backs, low, shining straight down
Oxford Street. And I'm watching them pour out of the
tube, wave after wave. The shopworkers, the office
workers. Another day for them. The newspaper. Work.
Coffee from the machine. Just like yesterday. And the day
before. And the day before that.

But not for me. I felt like a kid on his birthday. The day
belongs to me. It's D-Day.

CASS: D-Day?

BILLY: Look at them soppy bastards, Cass. What do you see? I
see people, they fuck themself. The bus is full, the machine
don't work, THEY FUCK THEMSELF!

CASS: Billy, don't make a scene.

BILLY: War is a thing, Cass. I can fucking taste it.

CASS: Let's go home.

BILLY: I'm bristling, Cass, don't touch me. I am fucking alive.

CASS: You're over-tired.

BILLY: YOU MUGS!

CASS: I'm over-tired.

BILLY: No surrender, no retreat. Not till the day my brother
comes home, walks in the door, laughing at me. When I
hear him laugh, that's when I stop. I'll give them
REMEMBRANCE!

NCO: Guard of Honour, slow march.

(*The* GUARD OF HONOUR *escorts Bobby's coffin covered with a Union Jack to the ship's rail, as* BILLY *speaks to the audience.*)

BILLY: (*Displaying a medal*) South Atlantic Campaign Medal, posthumous. It came through the post in a jiffy bag. Julie gave it to me. And I give it back to the country. A land fit for heroes. (*Throws it away with all his might.*) What did you expect? GRATITUDE?

PADRE: They shall not grow old
    as we that are left grow old.
    Age shall not weary them
    nor the years condemn.
    At the going down of the sun,
    and in the morning,
    we will remember them.

RESPONSE: We will remember them.

NCO: Guard of Honour, reverse arms.
    (*The Bosun's whistle is sounded as the coffin is tilted and slipped into the sea. Then silence.*)

PADRE: The legion of the living salutes the legion of the dead.

RESPONSE: We will not break faith with ye.

BILLY: We will not break faith with ye.
    (*A volley of three shots is fired into the air. A shower of red poppy petals falls.*)

SECOND HALF

BILLY: (*With pram; sings:*)
> The grand old Duke of York
> He had ten thousand men
> He marched them up to the top of the hill
> And he marched them down again.

Typical fucking northerner.

Go to sleep. Go to sleep. I'm here. I'm here.

(*To the audience*) This is a fair old pram, this is. Good suspension. No mildew, no rust. Look at that chrome. That's well looked after, that is. Got it on the old never-never. Julie was all for second-hand, but not me, no way. Not second-hand, not for that kid. I'll go without meself, I don't mind. The kid comes first.

(*To the baby*) Ssh. Go to sleep, go to sleep. (*Suddenly vicious*) GO TO SLEEP!

What am I doing? I lost my . . . I lost my temper. Shit. What's the matter with me? I could of . . .

Ssh. Go to sleep. I'm sorry, I didn't mean it. I didn't mean it, I didn't mean it.

(*To the audience*) It's a thin line I walk between love and hate. Sometimes I think (I don't know) they must be the same thing. Because I love this country, even now. But time and time again it has shit on me, and for no other reason. So tell me this: what do I teach the kid? Eh? What? (*The passenger deck of Southampton–Santander ferry. Somewhere in the Bay of Biscay.*)

I stood on the deck of the ferry that day and I dreamed I was my brother, leaving Southampton, watching the white cliffs disappear in the mist. And in that moment I understood there was no going back. I gave no thought to danger. I gave no thought to right and wrong. It felt like I was sleepwalking.

GHOST: Warm night.

BILLY: Yes.

GHOST: We're going to have a storm.

BILLY: You reckon?

GHOST: I'm telling you. We are sailing down the throat of some
    rattling heavy seas.

BILLY: Good. I like a storm.

GHOST: You know where we are?

BILLY: No.

GHOST: This is the Bay of Biscay, this is:
    from Ushant to Finisterre
    these waters that the winds distress
    conceal a graveyard. Look around you:
    these horizons are the last
    that countless thousand men have seen.
    A mile or two beneath our keel
    they keep their wealth
    and feed the fishes.

    (*The* GHOST *is gone, his voice remaining.*)

BILLY: Bobby?

VOICE: Riches mock my bones.

BILLY: Bobby!

VOICE: Hush! Remember me.
    I'll drink your health – five fathom deep.

BILLY: I heard a sound like ripping canvas,
    water rushing in my ear . . .
    my mind was torn. He took my hand.
    And, hand in hand, we rode to hell.

    (CASS *enters.*)

CASS: Billy. . . !

BILLY: Huh?

CASS: Guess who I just seen?

BILLY: What? Who?

CASS: Guess.

BILLY: Harry Kellerway.

CASS: Yeah.

BILLY: Good old Harry.

CASS: How did you know?

BILLY: Love your enemies, Cass. Keep them close.

CASS: What?

BILLY: We're in for some rough fucking weather. Feel that swell. You'll need your sea legs.

CASS: Uh–hu. You all right?

BILLY: Fighting fit, Cass. Fighting fit.

CASS: Good.

BILLY: Why?

CASS: Nothing. Just asking.

BILLY: So. Harry Kellerway.

CASS: Yeah. He's in the bar . . .

BILLY: Leave me alone now, Cass. I need to think.

CASS: Sure.

BILLY: Cass . . .

CASS: What?

BILLY: (*Hesitates.*) Nothing.

(CASS *moves along the deck.* KENNO *runs to the rail and heaves.* MAL *strolls over.*)

MAL: Boring, innit?

KENNO: What?

MAL: The sea.

KENNO: I want to die.

CASS: Cheer up, Kenno. It's early days.

KENNO: Great. I can hardly contain myself.

MAL: We had noticed.

(TERRY *enters.*)

TERRY: You seen below? They got a buffet. Eat all you want for five quid. They got steak and chips and Brussels sprouts and apple pie and custard. You just stack it on your plate as much as you can eat. What you looking at, Kenno?

KENNO: Nothing.

MAL: He's concentrating.

TERRY: On what?

KENNO: Terry. Please don't talk to me.

TERRY: This is immaculate, innit? I never been on a boat before. I never been south of Bromley, me. Reckon they're expecting us?

MAL: Course they are. We're world famous.

CASS: Yeah. Everyone's heard of England.

TERRY: Who fancies swimming the last mile?

MAL: You must be joking. The water's poison. Full of used johnnies and turds and that. Got no hygiene, the dagos. Three rules. Don't drink the water, don't eat the food and don't breathe the air.

CASS: And remember. Stick together. We're a team. We work as a team.

BILLY: Who sez?

CASS: I do.

(HARRY *enters*.)

HARRY: That's the spirit, Kenno. Keep chucking it up. Only, when you see a round black bit, bite hard and swallow, cos that's your arsehole.

(*He laughs alone*.)

All right, boys? Hello, Billy. Ready for the off, then, are we? I am raring, fucking raring. COME ON YOU WHITES! Oh yes. I tell you: them dozy cunts will not know what has hit them. All the England is on this tub. It's packed to the port-holes with naughty chaps, with only one idea between them. I don't have to draw you a diagram, do I?

TERRY: Switch off, knucklebrain.

HARRY: What was that? I heard a noise. I must of imagined it. All right, Billy? Have you got the thing?

BILLY: What thing?

HARRY: You know what thing.

BILLY: I don't know what you mean.

HARRY: Yes you do.

BILLY: I don't know what you're talking here.

TERRY: What thing, Billy?

BILLY: NO FUCKING THING! ALL RIGHT?

HARRY: My mistake. I brought the subject up I shouldn't of. There is no thing. Very wise, Billy. Discretion is the better part of valour. Say no more.

BILLY: Fuck off, Harry.

HARRY: What I really wanted to say, Billy . . . (can we talk?) . . . listen. No, listen. I heard about your brother (listen to me: hear me out) and I just wanted to say, Billy, if there's anything I can do . . .

BILLY: There's nothing you can do.

HARRY: Will you just listen to me, one moment: I think there
is.

BILLY: There's nothing anyone can do.

HARRY: You're not listening to me, Billy: I think there is. I
think there is something we can do. Now hear this: we had
our disagreements, let's not deny it. But I say that is
history. I say that life goes on. I say that revenge is sweet.
There. I've said it. (*Slight pause.*) It's what you're thinking.

BILLY: What are you, a mind-reader?

HARRY: It's human nature.

BILLY: I'm different. Cass!

CASS: What?

BILLY: Let's get some scran. I fancy a bite.

HARRY: First things first, I quite agree. An army marches on its
stomach, as Winston said.

CASS: Napoleon.

HARRY: Eh?

CASS: It was Napoleon. Not Churchill.

HARRY: Are you trying to be funny? I'm not a cunt, you know.

CASS: I never said you was, Harry.

HARRY: As long as that is understood. Because I know what I'm
talking about. And I'm talking about Sir Winston fucking
Churchill! Right?

CASS: Whatever you say.

HARRY: Don't contradict me!

CASS: I was agreeing with you.

HARRY: Well I don't like your tone!

(*A thunderclap. The ship lurches.*)

BILLY: Nice one.

HARRY: (Shit.) I'm going in.

BILLY: What's the matter? It's funfair time.

HARRY: Rainwater stains. I've just had this suit dry-cleaned.

(*A thunderclap.* BILLY *whoops.* KENNO *moans.*)

Listen: this is the last thing I will say to you: any time you
boys need a decent meal, come to the Hotel del Mar, put it
on my account. See? I got a forgiving heart, Billy. We'll
talk again, you and me.

(HARRY *goes. Rolling thunder.*)

BILLY: Bosh! you roaring hurricanoes!
 soul-intrepid ambuscadoes!
 make Surf City look like Blackpool.
 Beat the vaulted darkling air
 you drum battalions lunatic.
 Gun it! Give me chaos! Thrill me!
 Scare the living shit out of me:
 elements, I challenge you!
 (*Sings:*) 'Rule Britannia, Britannia . . .' sing up, boys, sing
 up! What's the matter, you bunch of sighs?
GHOST: (*Rising from the sea*) I must have the gentleman to haul
 and draw with the mariner, and the mariner with the
 gentleman. I would know him that would refuse to set his
 hand to a rope. I know there is not any such here. You
 come, then, of your own free will: on you it depends to
 make the voyage renowned or to end a reproach to our
 country and a laughing-stock to the enemy. Let us show
 ourselves to be all of a company.
 (*Campsite. San Sebastian. Night. Cicadas sing.* THE LADS
 enter and drop to the ground, exhausted.)
CASS: Come on, Billy. This is a good spot.
KENNO: Nice and soft.
TERRY: I could sleep on broken glass, I'm that shagged.
 (*Pause. They lie there.*)
CASS: I hope there ent no snakes.
 (ALL *leap to their feet instantly, except* CASS, *who is laughing.*)
 Mugs.
BILLY: Let's get this fucking tent up.
CASS: Come on, men. You're in the Army now, and you're
 gonna take Bilbao.
 (*They begin to put up the tent.*)
TERRY: (*Slaps his arm.*) Ow!
CASS: Mosquitoes.
TERRY: Pesky little buggers. This Spain's a right hole, innit?
 It's all countryside.
KENNO: It's like a bleeding sauna. I'm honking like a yid.
MAL: I'm parched.
TERRY: Have to suck pebbles. Like the Foreign Legion.

61

KENNO: Dunno how they stick it, the dagos. *I* couldn't live here. All right for holidays, but living here . . . they can keep it.

CASS: You get used to things.

TERRY: Suppose it's what you're born to, innit?

MAL: I had a mate joined the Legion.

CASS: Oh yeah?

MAL: Yeah.

CASS: What did he reckon to it?

MAL: He sez it's like watching Millwall. You don't notice the violence after a bit.

TERRY: I thought of joining the Legion once.

KENNO: To forget.

TERRY: Forget what? Nothing *to* forget.

MAL: They ought to bring back National Service. Give us something to do.

KENNO: I'll tell you what you boys need. Three months in a detention centre. Makes a man of you, that does. Teaches you self-discipline. That's what it taught me. How to fight and how to fight proper. I was a fucking wanker before I went inside. Just like you, Terry.

TERRY: Stop picking on me, will you.

KENNO: Who's picking on you? I'm only saying.

TERRY: Everyone is. (*Slaps his arm.*) Ow!

BILLY: Whose mags are these? *Sadie Stern? Swish?*

KENNO: Oi! Give 'em here!

BILLY: Kenno, really.

KENNO: Who said you could touch my things?

CASS: It's all right, Kenno. Your secret is safe with us.

TERRY: He's gone red.

KENNO: Fuck off.

TERRY: He has. He's gone red.

KENNO: Fuck off, Terry.

CASS: You find out about people, these conditions.

MAL: Let's have a shuftie.

BILLY: Phrase book? Is this yours and all?

KENNO: Yeah. Might be handy.

BILLY: (*Throws it away.*) Let them speak English.

62

CASS: What happens if they don't?

BILLY: That's their problem.

TERRY: (*Slaps his arm.*) Ow! Why am I the only one gets bit? It ent fucking fair.

CASS: It must be your animal magnetism, Tel.

TERRY: I lost me job over this caper.

BILLY: What you expect? A medal?

TERRY: Them bastards up the works, they wouldn't give me the time off.

CASS: Chronic.

TERRY: Well, I'll tell you this. They can stuff their job. It was fucking boring anyway.

KENNO: I went on the sick.

TERRY: You what?

KENNO: On the sick, me.

TERRY: Shit. I never thought of that.

MAL: Me, I sacrificed my whole future life of married bliss to come out here. Not that there was much in it. I'd of gone mad if I'd stayed at home.

CASS: Poor Christine.

MAL: Sod that dozy bitch. I tried to explain but she refuses to understand. The World Cup don't mean shit to her. She likes Chelsea one week, Tottenham the next . . . drives me up the wall. So I told her straight. The lads need me. I'm putting my country first.

KENNO: What she say?

MAL: She didn't say nothing. She just hit me with a ironing board. Fucking bruised all up me back.

CASS: So the wedding's off, then.

MAL: Clashes with England vee Czechoslovakia.

KENNO: Her old man'll murder you.

MAL: Her old man's already on the plane to Bilbao.

THE LADS: (*Sing:*)

> My old man said be an England fan
> And don't dilly dally on the way
> We'll take Bilbao and every fucker in it
> We'll take Bilbao in under half a minute
> With hatchets and hammers

63

And half-a-dozen spanners
La la la la . . .

BILLY: Look at all them bleeding stars.

TERRY: Where?

BILLY: Terry. In the sky.

TERRY: Oh yeah.

KENNO: 'Oh yeah.'

TERRY: There's billions.

MAL: Never get this many at home.

TERRY: Christ.

CASS: What?

TERRY: Makes you feel small, don't it?

CASS: What?

TERRY: The universe.

CASS: It don't make me feel small.

TERRY: What's that red one? Blink blink blink blink.

KENNO: Aeroplane.

TERRY: Oh yeah. What's that noise?

MAL: What noise?

TERRY: Like frogs.

KENNO: That's crickets.

TERRY: What they doing, you reckon?

KENNO: Scratching their heads.

MAL: I hate cricket.

TERRY: It's dinnertime at home. I wonder what they're having.

KENNO: You got food on the brain, you have.

TERRY: Me stomach thinks me throat's been cut.

KENNO: It will be if you don't shut up. I gave you my bag of
    crisps.

TERRY: Crisps ent filling. I need something proper. What's
    Spanish food like?

MAL: Dagos eat horses.

KENNO: Nah. That's the frogs.

MAL: Nah. Frogs eat frogs. That's how they get the name, see.
    Stands to reason, don't it?

TERRY: How could you eat a frog?

CASS: You'll eat anything if you're hungry.

MAL: Eat dago food tonight, you'll have an arsehole like a fresh bullet wound in the morning.

KENNO: I could murder a portion of chips.

TERRY: Me taste buds is tingling.

KENNO: And I don't mean Spanish chips, mind you. I mean English chips.

TERRY: In the circumstances, I couldn't give a fuck. Chips is chips.

KENNO: No, Terry. That is where you are wrong. Some chips, Terry, is crusty brown on the outside and steaming hot on a crisp cold night. Some chips come wrapped in Page Three, stained with vinegar and smothered in that much brown sauce it brings tears to your eyes. No, Terry. There is chips and there is chips.

TERRY: Curry sauce.

KENNO: What?

TERRY: Chips with curry sauce.

KENNO: Yeah.

MAL: And a huge glistening saveloy protruding turd-like from the wrapper.

TERRY: It's enough to send shivers down your spine.

CASS: Billy.

BILLY: What?

CASS: The troops is peckish.

BILLY: Well, that's easy, innit? You only had to say.

(*The raid. A farmhouse and yard. The yard is surrounded by a high wire fence. Two* MEN *sit in the porch to the house. They are drinking wine, singing, arguing in Spanish, perhaps over cards. Pantomime:* THE LADS *steal a chicken from the yard.*

A clearing in the woods. THE LADS *are gathered around the stolen chicken.*)

KENNO: I ent killing it, I can tell you that for nothing.

CASS: (*To* TERRY) What are you doing?

TERRY: See if it likes chocolate. Come on, chicken. Come on, chicken.

(*The chicken pecks* TERRY.)

OW! See that? Fucking thing bit me.

CASS: Come on, Kenno. You drew the short straw.

KENNO: I ent doing it and that is final.

BILLY: Look, all you got to do is put one hand there, and one hand there and . . .

CASS: . . . wring its neck.

BILLY: . . . wring its neck.

CASS: (*'Tommy Cooper'*) Just like that.

KENNO: I don't feel so hungry.

TERRY: (*Trying again*) Come on, chicken. That's the boy. That's the boy.

KENNO: I think Terry ought to do it.

TERRY: What?

KENNO: Terry ought to do it. He started it.

TERRY: I did not.

MAL: It was your idea, Tel.

TERRY: It wasn't. It was Billy's idea.

BILLY: You wanted something to eat, son.

TERRY: Yeah but . . .

BILLY: Yeah but, yeah but! Kill it, you nonce!

TERRY: I can't! It's alive!

BILLY: It's only a fucking chicken.

TERRY: Still got feelings, ent it?

BILLY: You've ate chicken before, ent you?

TERRY: Yeah but . . .

BILLY: Well then. Listen, I have worked six months in a slaughterhouse, I have put bolts through the heads of living cows, so don't you tell me about they got feelings. Christ, if everyone was like you, we'd all be dead. Survival, Terry. It's a law. Understand?

TERRY: Yeah.

BILLY: Then do the business.

(TERRY *approaches the chicken.*)

TERRY: Here, chicken. Come on, chicken. That's the boy. One hand there, and one hand there, and . . . (*Recoils.*) IT MOVED!

MAL: Fucking Ada.

TERRY: I can't do it, lads. Not with me bare hands. I'm sorry but I just can't hack it.

CASS: We won't have to kill it at this rate. It'll die of old age.

BILLY: Bunch of sighs.

66

CASS: Why don't you do it, Billy?

TERRY: Yeah. Why don't you do it, Billy?

BILLY: I could do it. I know I could do it. I've done it before, I
could do it again. I'm used to it. I just thought someone
else might want a go.

ALL: No, no. It's all right, Billy. He's all yours.

BILLY: You want me to do it?

ALL: Yeah.

BILLY: OK.

(*He grabs the chicken.* TERRY *can't look.* BILLY *hesitates.*)

CASS: What's the matter, Billy?

BILLY: It's looking at me.

KENNO: Close your eyes, Billy. Close your eyes.

(BILLY *closes his eyes. He hesitates, opens one eye.*)

BILLY: Fuck. I can't.

TERRY: (Thank Christ for that.)

BILLY: I swear to God it was looking at me.

MAL: (Jesus wept.)

KENNO: All right then. Who's next?

(*They look at* MAL.)

MAL: You know what I think? We should of went with Harry.

TERRY: What?

MAL: We should of fucking went with Harry. He's all right,
Harry is. He would of done all right by us. I mean this is
just silly. What are we, fucking Venture Scouts?

CASS: Is that your attitude, Malcolm?

MAL: Yes, as it happens. That is my attitude. My attitude is
there is no toilet paper in a forest. Only fucking trees.

CASS: You know how to find the Hotel del Mar?

MAL: No problem.

CASS: Well then.

(*Pause.*)

MAL: Kenno?

KENNO: What?

MAL: Coming?

TERRY: You ent really going, are you?

MAL: Billy?

BILLY: It's your business. I don't interfere.

67

(*Pause.* MAL *goes.*)

TERRY: He ent really going, is he?

CASS: I think he is, Terry.

TERRY: He don't mean it. He'll be back.

BILLY: Well, I ent waiting for him. Come on. Let's chip.

(BILLY *and* KENNO *move off.*)

CASS: Come on, Terry. Let's go.

TERRY: What about the chicken?

CASS: Leave it.

TERRY: On its own?

CASS: Terry!

(TERRY *follows* CASS. *The chicken remains.*

The scene is now a restaurant. THE LADS *sit at one table, drunk. A* MAN *sits alone at another. There is a* SPANISH WAITER.)

THE LADS: (*Sing:*)

　　What shall we do with the Argentinians
　　Bomb bomb Buenos Aires!

　　Rule Britannia, Britannia rules the waves
　　Britons never never never shall be slaves

BILLY: (*To* WAITER) Oi! Bollocks! Over here. Another bottle of firewater, pronto. Savvy?

WAITER: Si, señor.

KENNO: Oi! Mush! Where's the action in this town?

WAITER: The. . . ?

KENNO: I said where's the fucking action! What's the matter? Are you deaf?

CASS: Kenno, leave it out. The man is working shifts. Have a fucking heart.

KENNO: He's a waiter, he should speak English.

CASS: What, like you do?

KENNO: It's part of the job. It shows respect. (*To the* WAITER) Respect? Yes?

WAITER: Yes . . .

KENNO: What's that in Spanish?

WAITER: I . . .

BILLY: They probably ent got a word for it. I wouldn't be

68

surprised.

KENNO: Here are. I know Spanish. Listen: Malvinas Inglaterra. Understand?

WAITER: Yes.

BILLY: I'll bet he does. Now get the bill.

WAITER: The. . . ?

BILLY: THE BILL THE BILL THE BILL!

KENNO: If he ent deaf he must be stupid.

CASS: What's the matter with you two? We've had good service here tonight.

BILLY: Don't talk to me, Cass. Do not talk to me. (*To the* MAN) What you looking at? What you looking at, eh?

CASS: (*To the* MAN) He's had too much wine.

BILLY: (*To the* MAN) You looking at me? You looking at me, cunt?

MAN: (*Northern*) Mind if I join you? I can't stick drinking on me own.

BILLY: You're English. He's English.

MAN: Aye.

BILLY: Why didn't you say nothing? Sit down, you cunt, sit down. Have some fucking wine. Us English got to stick together. Ent we? Eh? Where you from?

MAN: Leeds.

BILLY: You can't help where you're born, can you?

MAN: No.

KENNO: We're Millwall.

MAN: Millwall.

BILLY: Fucking right we are.

MAN: Reckon our chances, do you?

KENNO: What?

MAN: The football.

KENNO: Course.

MAN: Win?

KENNO: Could be.

MAN: The World Cup?

KENNO: Yeah. Why not?

MAN: England never win shit.

(*Pause.*)

69

TERRY: Outside chance.

MAN: Listen to Brian Clough here.

TERRY: Outside chance, I reckon.

MAN: Be lucky to make Phase Two.

KENNO: You reckon?

MAN: England? The Millwall of the world.

KENNO: The what?

MAN: And we invented the fucking game.

KENNO: I know that.

MAN: Who invented football?

KENNO: England.

MAN: Fucking right. Fucking England. Football's
mother fucking country.

KENNO: Yeah.

MAN: Eh?

KENNO: That's right.

MAN: I ask you.

(*The* WAITER *returns with the bill.*)

CASS: (*To the* WAITER) Listen. I'm sorry about . . .

WAITER: No, please. We know the English.

BILLY: (*Reads:*) Four steak and chips. Four bottles of Bull's
Blood. Fifty thousand pesetas. What's that in English?

CASS: About a score.

KENNO: Pesetas ent worth shit. Everyone's a millionaire out
here.

BILLY: (*Counting out £5 notes*) There are. Twenty quid. That
should do you.

WAITER: Sorry. This . . .

BILLY: What's the problem?

CASS: It's all right. I've got traveller's cheques.

BILLY: Put 'em away. What's wrong with good English money?
What's wrong with pounds sterling? That is hard cash.
Take it or leave it.

WAITER: (Oh my God. The bloody English.) Excuse me.
(*The* WAITER *goes.*)

MAN: Happen he's gone to call the police.

BILLY: I couldn't give a fuck.

MAN: A word of advice, lad. Spanish cops are crazy men. They just wade into the English. They'll batter you for crossing the road.

TERRY: Maybe we ought to piss off.

BILLY: Stay put.

MAN: The English, they're a fucking joke out here.

BILLY: What you mean?

MAN: Well, England's gone. The whole fucking country. Gone to the dogs. And you know why?

BILLY: Why?

MAN: People like you.

(*Pause.*)

BILLY: You what?

MAN: I come here for a quiet drink. And what do I get? Embarrassed. Ashamed to be an Englishman. You're worse than the sodding Krauts, you lot.

KENNO: In this country we can do what we like. Whose side are you on anyway?

MAN: Don't you come it with me, son. I'll break every bone in your body.

CASS: Slow down . . .

KENNO: You can't blame us for being patriotic. There's a fucking war on, you know.

MAN: Oh yes. It's been in all the papers.

(*The* MAN *rolls up his sleeve to show a tattoo.*)

See that?

KENNO: Yeah.

MAN: What's it say?

KENNO: Three Para.

MAN: You want to argue with it?

KENNO: No.

MAN: What?

KENNO: No.

MAN: I should hope not. (*Slight pause.*) You know what a paratrooper is? I'll tell you. In Crossmaglen or the Ardoyne, a paratrooper is one of two things. He is either scared shitless, or bored shitless. On foot patrol, scared shitless. Back to barracks: bored shitless. Foot patrol: scared shitless. Back to barracks: bored shitless. Get the idea? A tour of duty is four months. It's a great life, lad. It's good crack scraping your oppo off pavement. It's a reet laugh getting shot at by twelve-year-old micks. You like blood, do you? You should join the fucking Professionals, son. Do we understand each other? Are we speaking the same language?

(KENNO *nods.*)

I came here on holiday. I brought the wife. I don't want to hear any more of that shit.

(*The* MAN *goes.*)

BILLY: (*Sings:*)

    The Argies they went to the Falklands
    They said that they wanted ruck
    So the Argies went in
    And the English moved in
    And kicked all the Argies to fuck.

(*An* ARMED POLICEMAN *enters. The scene changes to the corridor of a police station.* MAL *stands spreadeagled against a wall.* THE LADS *are ushered in by the* COP.)

KENNO: Well well. Look who it ent.

CASS: Hello, Malcolm.

MAL: Hello, boys.

BILLY: For once in his life, he's early.

MAL: I got fucking lost in the fucking woods, I asked a fucking copper the fucking way and he fucking well arrested me. What a fucking liberty. I'm a fucking British citizen.

(*The* COP *strikes* MAL.)

COP: Silencio!

MAL: Me arms hurt.

COP: Basta.

BILLY: (*To the audience*) I've got the gun bandaged to me chest. Soon as I've seen the dago tooled up likewise, I know it's off. I know it's really off. And me heart is knocking me ribs so hard I am sure everyone can hear it. But you didn't move a muscle . . .

CASS: Me nose itches.

COP: Silencio!

BILLY: And you didn't breathe a word . . .

72

TERRY: I want a slash.

COP: Tu hablas quando yo digo. Comprende? Comprende?

TERRY: What?

COP: Diga, si, señor. Si, señor.

TERRY: Si, señor.

(*The* COP *laughs.*)

BILLY: (*To the audience*) They'd batter you for so much as blinking. Funny thing is: they never bothered searching us. They was too busy taking the piss. It could never of happened in England. No discipline, the continentals. No idea at all.

COP: Tu madre era puta. Una gran puta di mierda. Comprende?

TERRY: Si, señor.

COP: (*Laughs.*) 'Si, señor.' Malvinas son Argentinas. Comprende?

TERRY: Si, señor.

COP: 'Si, señor.'

(*Pause.*)

TERRY: Señor. I want to go to the toilet, señor.

COP: I don't speak English.

TERRY: The toilet, señor. Please.

COP: No.

TERRY: I got to have a slash, señor.

COP: Silencio.

TERRY: I'm gonna piss meself!

COP: SILENCIO!

TERRY: I GOTTA HAVE A FUCKING SLASH YOU CUNT!

COP: BRUTOS!

(*The* COP *beats* TERRY *to the ground. He groans.*)

TERRY: Oh no. Oh no.

(*The* COP *picks* TERRY *up. He is in tears.*)

CASS: You cunt.

COP: Basta.

(*Silence.* TERRY *sobs. Then* CASS *starts humming 'Rule Britannia'.* BILLY *starts singing the words.*)

Digo, basta!

(*All at once* THE LADS *are singing 'Rule Britannia' loud and clear. The* COP *lays into them with a baton. The singing dries up. A door opens. Someone calls, in Spanish:* All right. Let the English go. Charges have been dropped. THE LADS *are released.*

 The scene is now the steps of the police station. HARRY *is waiting for them – Bermuda shorts and Hawaiian shirt.*)

HARRY: Hello, boys. You look worn out. I hope they ent been mistreating you.

BILLY: Kellerway. I might of known.

HARRY: Bad news travels fast.

CASS: And where there's shit there's a spoon.

HARRY: Well? Ent you gonna thank me? I saved your fucking bacon.

MAL: I told you, didn't I?

CASS: Yeah. The strokes he pulls. He's magic.

MAL: Dunno how you manage it, Harry. My life.

HARRY: Graft, how do you think? You got to know how to deal with people. A policeman is only a human being. Let's get you into a taxi. We're going to my hotel.

 (*The scene is now a hotel terrace, by the swimming pool. Piped Muzak. A cocktail bar and* BARMAN.)

A single room, we are talking forty pounds a night. And that is before anything else. It's impressive, huh?

MAL: Yeah.

HARRY: It impresses the fuck out of me. You ever eat a lobster?

MAL: No.

HARRY: You have not lived.

BILLY: You own this place?

HARRY: Not exactly, no. The situation is this: I am planning to acquire an interest in it. You can't invade a country, buy it. You need a wash?

BILLY: Later, Harry.

HARRY: I don't feel human till I brush my teeth in the morning.

CASS: I can believe that.

HARRY: You will not believe the bathroom. You will not believe the marble they got. I mean it is real. And that is the kind of place this is. And I intend to have a piece of it. What are you drinking? Martini? Pina colada? (*To* CASS) By the way. I looked it up. It was Churchill. I was right.

74

CASS: Where did you look it up?

HARRY: What?

CASS: Where did you look it up?

HARRY: What the fuck does it matter? I looked it up! I was right!

TERRY: What's a Pina colada?

HARRY: Make yourselves at home, boys. The bar is free. The sun is shining. This is the life, eh? Fuck me, yes. I'm thinking of stopping here for good, I am. I mean, England, well . . . England's gone. The interest rates don't favour small business. Me, I want to expand. I'm an Englishman of the blood. All Englishmen want to expand. It's as natural as pissing to us. Go south, young man, go south.

CASS: West.

HARRY: West, south, what the fuck. But don't get me wrong on this: England is still the greatest country in the world. And when I think of Bermondsey, a tear comes to my eye. But the trouble with the English is, they cannot think big. They are a nation of shopkeepers. (*To* CASS) Who said that?

CASS: Don't ask me.

HARRY: I got him! I got him!

CASS: Look at that: I've made him happy.

HARRY: But seriously, Billy, joking apart: in twenty years (mark my words) England will be a member of the fucking Third World. What do you think of the Common Market? It is a piece of shit. It doesn't stand a chance. And you know why? Because a nation has got its culture, Billy. Do you know what I mean when I say that?

BILLY: Culture, yes.

HARRY: It's culture, Billy, is its independence, and its freedom, to go into other likewise nations. With a view to securing an honest profit. Does that make sense to you?

BILLY: Uh–hu.

HARRY: It makes sense to me. Do you like this shirt?

BILLY: It's . . .

HARRY: What's your chest size?

BILLY: I don't know.

HARRY: Can we talk?

BILLY: What?

75

HARRY: Listen: this country is wide open. The Spanish, they are soft. They are lazy, they are dopey. They are cowards. But vicious. And cruel to animals. You ever see a bullfight? They are also deceitful, and will cut your throat for thirty bob. But if you raise your voice to them, they cry like babies. And another thing: they treat their women like shit. Which is one thing I will not stand for.

BILLY: What are you saying here?

HARRY: Billy: it was one of this scum what killed your brother. (*Pause.*)

CASS: Which one?

HARRY: What?

CASS: You're so wise: which one was it pulled the trigger?

HARRY: Now I've heard everything.

CASS: We're gonna find some criminals, let's go about it businesslike. Now tell me: where does he live? What are his movements?

HARRY: (*To* BILLY) I hope you're listening to this.

CASS: I'm waiting, Harry.

HARRY: Who gives a toss which one it was? Who honestly cares? That dago cunt what pulled the trigger, did he stop and ask himself: is Bobby Jarvis fair game? Did he? No! Then why the fuck should we? A spic is a spic. Any one of them will do.

CASS: What do you think, Billy?

BILLY: I think . . . Harry might have a point.

CASS: 'Any one of them will do.'

BILLY: Yes.

CASS: How about me then?

BILLY: You ent a spic.

CASS: What am I, then? An 'Englishman'? You reckon Harry looks at me, he sees an 'Englishman'? Look at me, Billy. What am I? How far away from you must I stand before you see me what I am? A hundred yards, am I still your friend?

BILLY: I don't understand . . . what you're saying.

CASS: For fuck sake Billy: you are terrifying me.

BILLY: Why?

76

CASS: Can't you see? Kick a dago, kick a nigger – what's the fucking odds?

HARRY: I couldn't of put it better myself.

CASS: Billy, this man is talking murder.

BILLY: Wait a minute, both of you. I can't think straight, I . . .

HARRY: It's simple, Billy. It's so simple I could cry.

CASS: You know what is simple? A baseball bat is simple.

BILLY: STOP! STOP! (*Pause.*) One at a time.

HARRY: I want to introduce you to some people.

BILLY: Who?

HARRY: Some people I know.

BILLY: Who are they?

HARRY: The Snipers. The Inter City. The Huyton Baddies. The Yids. The Gooners. The Mancs. The Scallies. The hard cases. The crack ruckers. The élite of England's fighting crews. They're all yours, Billy. All you got to do is say the word. We'll start the ruck to end all rucks. Kick blood and shit out of Johnny Dago.

BILLY: I . . . I . . .

HARRY: It's what you want.

CASS: (*To* HARRY) What's in it for you?

HARRY: Nothing. Absolutely not a thing. I want to do one thing in my life for love instead of money.

CASS: You got a heart of gold, Harry. You ought to rip it out your chest. It might be worth a bit. (*To* BILLY) Can we talk?

BILLY: (*To* HARRY) Excuse me a moment.

HARRY: Be my guest.

(BILLY *and* CASS *confer.*)

BILLY: What?

CASS: That man is your enemy.

BILLY: A man without enemies is a man without friends. Know what I mean?

CASS: No.

BILLY: Listen. I have seen my brother.

CASS: When?

BILLY: I have seen my brother.

CASS: Give it less thought, Billy.

BILLY: Listen, Cass: the exact moment of his death, what was I doing? I was probably down the boozer with you lot.

CASS: Yes.

BILLY: I was probably watching the telly.

CASS: That's it, see.

BILLY: There's nothing I could of done, is there?

CASS: No.

BILLY: Well, there is something I can do now.

CASS: It won't bring him back, will it?

BILLY: I know that.

CASS: Then what the fuck can be the use?

BILLY: Don't push your luck, Cass.

CASS: All I'm saying . . .

BILLY: I ent interested!

CASS: You should be. It's your brother we're talking about.

BILLY: That's right. My brother. So it ent your place to say nothing.

CASS: What? This is Cass talking. Your friend.

BILLY: A friend? What's a friend? I had a brother! No one takes his place!

CASS: Oh Billy. How can you say that?

BILLY: Do not, do not, do not, CROSS ME!
    (*Slight pause.*)

CASS: Your brother . . . he would not of reckoned this. He had a word for Kellerway.

HARRY: And what was that?

CASS: Traitor.

HARRY: Muzzle that coon, Jarvis.
    (*Slight pause.*)

CASS: Billy . . . this piece of nothing . . .

BILLY: Do what he sez.

CASS: What?

BILLY: Can it!

CASS: You're telling me. . . ?

BILLY: Shut the fuck up!
    (*Slight pause.*)

CASS: NOW YOU HAVE BROKE MY FUCKING PATIENCE! What am I, your slave, you give me orders? What am I, your dog,

78

you can kick me? Am I your wife? Your nigger? Your property?

BILLY: I put my dick on the line for you.

CASS: Some dick! some line! what a fucking hero! What about me? you think about that? the things I did for you? all those times, Billy, all those times . . . you talk, I listen, I share your grief, I do what I can, I'm always fucking THERE! Did you never notice that? Huh? Billy: when did you ever come to my house? once? twice? in ten fucking years? I gave you all the time I had; my own family took second place. And now this thing, this . . . 'friendship' I thought we had, it's a knife with no fucking handle. I've lost something, Billy – but don't you worry, it ent all that much. Ten years of my life, that's all. But not my fucking soul. (*Pause.*) This is it, Billy. We're finished, you and me. (*Pause.*) Ent you got nothing to say? (*Pause.*) Billy: you fight blindfold. What was Bobby? Was he a saint? I never saw his wings. But he was a good man. So now he's gone and what's the odds? They'll write it in the history books, another little war. He died for some fuckheads, they dance on his grave with serious faces. He was anyone: he was no one. Tell me, Billy. I want to know: what is there worth dying for? (*Pause.*)

BILLY: I can do without you, Cass. What's one man more or less? Anyone else bottling down?

MAL: I'm with you, Billy.

KENNO: Yeah. Me too. Come on, Cass. Give 'em one for Bobby. (CASS *spits. He turns to go.*)

BILLY: You cunt! You're finished, you cunt! You show your face down Millwall, you just try it! Your name is shit! Because you're out! You're fucking out for good, nigger! (CASS *comes back, faces* BILLY.)

CASS: And as for you, Jarvis: when you get home, if you ever see me walking your direction . . . cross the street. Before I see you. Mind how you go.
(CASS *goes. Pause.*)

HARRY: You find out who your friends are, don't you?

TERRY: You ent going to let him go, are you?

HARRY: Nature is strong, Billy. No use fighting it. The white man hates the black man. And the black man hates the white man and vice versa. Now let's not look for reasons in this. Because a reason is an excuse. The man who needs reasons is frightened to live. I make no excuses. I shit reasons. What does that make me, an idiot? No. It makes me strong.

BILLY: Yes. You're right.

HARRY: The white race has got to defend itself, Billy. And the best form of defence is attack.

TERRY: You ent gonna let him go, Billy? Out there? On his own? He could get killed. Someone might kill him.

BILLY: Who gives a shit?

(TERRY *goes*.)

HARRY: That kid is crazy.

(TERRY *wanders the streets of Bilbao looking for* CASS. *A crowd of Spaniards jeer him. In the distance a drum beats*.)

TERRY: Cass! Where are you? Cass!

(*The crowd begins to stone* TERRY.)

You cunts. You killed my friend, you cunts. Come and get it you . . . Come and get it! Come on! You want some? You want some?

(*He tries to advance. The drum beats louder*.)

'Rule Britannia, Britannia rules the . . .'

(*He falls. The* DRUMMER *arrives, wearing a black hood*.)

Cass! Where are you . . . where are you . . . where are you . . .

(*Blackout.* BILLY *appears, applying Union Jack face paint*.)

BILLY: (*Sings:*)

We'll take more care of you.

Fly the flag

Fly the flag . . .

These colours on my face I wore with pride, and not for camouflage. Like the Polish cavalry we're charging at tanks with a clatter of swords and a flag and a drum. We don't hide behind shit colour khaki! It feels good, it is a buzz to stand up straight and say FUCK YOU. And that's the truest thing you'll ever hear. Like this war paint: you ent got a face. Just a Union Jack. And you can do whatever the fuck you want to do.

(*A hospital intensive care unit.* TERRY *is in bed, comatose, connected to a monitoring machine.* CASS *sits by him.* BILLY *stands.*)

CASS: Terry. Terry. It's Cass. I'm here, Terry. Wake up. Wake up. Please wake up.

BILLY: He's sleeping. It's all right. Let him sleep it off. He'll wake up soon. TERRY!

CASS: Ssh. The other people.

BILLY: Who did this? Who did this? I'll . . .

(CASS *looks at him. Pause.*)

What you doing?

CASS: Holding his hand. It might help. I don't know.

BILLY: Mm.

CASS: All his vital signs are normal.

BILLY: Well, there you are then.

CASS: Yes.

BILLY: He won't half have a headache when he wakes up.

TERRY: (*Indistinct*) Stand your ground.

CASS: Sh.

BILLY: Wh – ?

CASS: Sh.

(*Pause.*)

TERRY: (*Indistinct*) Stand your ground.

CASS: 'Stand your ground.'

BILLY: What does he mean?

CASS: Terry. Terry.

BILLY: What does he mean, 'stand your ground'? (*Pause.*) They fucked him up. Those bastards.

CASS: We did, Billy. This is us. Now what am I gonna tell his mum?

(*The scene changes. Outside.* BILLY, HARRY *and the* GHOST.)

BILLY: I don't know where I fucking am. I don't know what to think of this.

GHOST: Your thoughts will cut you down to size.

BILLY: It's all right for you to talk.

HARRY: I ent said nothing.

GHOST: Conscience is a word that cowards use.

BILLY: You're well out of it, ent you?

HARRY: You what?

BILLY: Nothing, nothing.

HARRY: You feeling all right?

BILLY: Yeah, course. What happens now?

HARRY and GHOST: I give you the tools. You finish the job.

BILLY: One at a time for fuck sake.

HARRY: You what?

BILLY: Uuh . . .

HARRY: You sure you're. . . ?

BILLY: Course I fucking am. Now let's get on with it.

HARRY: OK. OK. Come with me.

HARRY and GHOST: I want you to meet some friends of mine.

BILLY: Yes.

GHOST: And I want you to understand –

HARRY: Any friend of mine is a friend of yours.

GHOST: On that you can rely.

BILLY: Right.

GHOST: Now watch this: SONS OF ENGLAND, ARISE!
    (*Historical tableau or procession:* KING, KNIGHT, PEASANT,
    PARA. *Fanfare and flags.*)

CHORALE: Always in the lives of great nations comes the
    moment of decision, comes the moment of destiny. And
    this nation again and again in the great hours of its fate has
    swept aside convention, has swept aside the little men of
    talk and of delay and has decided to follow men of
    movement, who say we go forward to action. Let who dare
    follow us in this hour!

KNIGHT: We are just plain-speaking soldiers.

KING: We are the death or glory boys.

PARA: I died up on Wireless Ridge
    bending to dimp my cigarette –
    he picked me out with infra-red,
    the sniper up on Wireless Ridge,
    the Argie with the Russian rifle.

KING: On the field of Agincourt
    we bobbed and thumped the bitch's bastards,

made them squeal like pigs in autumn.

KNIGHT: Autumn is the killing season,
    time to lay in meat for winter.

PARA: And now the winter is upon us,
    the winter of the Soul.

KNIGHT: I am the Quartermaster General.
    The time has come, the time for action –
    cook a broth with bone and water,
    thicken it with Spanish blood;
    roast their greasy hides for crackling,
    weave their hair in army blankets,
    cut their wedding rings off, melt them . . .
    who'll say Grace? the Army's feasting
    on the Army of the Dead.

PEASANT: It's thirsty bloody work, is slaughter.

PARA: Soldiers are like billy goats –
    they'll eat the webbing off their tunics.

KING: O noble English! mighty-hearted!
    half your force is adequate
    to blight the full-blown flower of Spain:
    the other half may lie a-bed.

PEASANT: (And dream of Blackpool in the rain.)

KNIGHT: London, pour out your citizens!

KING: Now all the youth of England are on fire!

KNIGHT: Account yourself a lucky man who dwells within the
    Wooden Walls of England, environed with a Great Ditch
    from all the world besides.

KING: We are a peace-loving people.

KNIGHT: But we can be a warlike nation!

PEASANT: Know what you fight for.
    Love what you know.
    Fear God.

    (*Pause.*)

BILLY: Who are you?

KNIGHT: In Life, there are two Armies.

KING: But the Army of the Dead is Legion.

BILLY: Souls of my ancestors, give me strength.

KNIGHT: God is on our side!

BILLY: How can we be sure?

KING: He speaks to us! WE WILL LIVE!
Cry God for Harry . . . !
(*He is shot in the eye with an arrow.*)

KNIGHT: The King is dead.

CHORALE: Long live the King!

PEASANT: (King of what? A nation of butchers?)

PARA: I am the Armourer; I thrive.
Give me your sword: I'll grind the edge
as sharp as a blade of grass.
Make a living, make a killing.
Life is a bowl of soup.

PEASANT: I died in Valparaiso,
fifteen hundred and forty-two.
The Spaniards caught us on the beach.
They cut off our hands, feet, noses and ears,
and tied us to trees to be tortured by flies
and other beasts.

KING: You, who levy war in the name of the Pope –
who is without authority from God or man:
a detestable shaveling, the right Antichrist –
You, who suckle the milk of the Roman Whore of
Babylon –
Before you – idolatrous barbarians! – I do protest:
if God give me life and leave, I mean to reap
some of your Harvest which you get out of the earth
and send into Spain to trouble all the world;
as God is my right and strength, I mean to halt
your bloody steps which blemish sweet Europa's face.

You dare to call me Pirate!
The use of the sea and air is common to all.
I'll board your Spanish galleons and you shall this day
be lighter of your illegal cargoes that you may
reach home the faster.
Or perhaps I'll hew your topmast
and send your dark sons down to the sunless deep
of the ocean to sleep amid sunken wrack and fishes.

You dare to call me Dragon!
I shall breathe fire upon your sails
and on your parachutes!

I AM A WARRY BASTARD, I AM!

Any questions?

PEASANT: What if we are defeated?

KING: What . . . if . . . we. . . ?

PEASANT: . . . are defeated.

KING: Defeat? The possibility does not exist!

PEASANT: I beseech you, in the bowels of Christ, think it
possible you may be mistaken.
(*Pause.*)

KING: I charge you with Mutiny,
High Treason and Witchcraft!

PEASANT: Witchcraft?

KING: I will make you shorter by the head.
What is the verdict of the Jury?

ALL: Guilty.

KING: You will be taken from this court
to a place of execution . . .

PEASANT: I don't want to die.

PARA: You should have thought of that before.

PEASANT: I don't want to die!

PARA: Nobody wants to die. Take it like a man, you nancy boy.

PEASANT: You're making a mistake.

PARA: Don't come the innocent with me, soldier. When you
signed up you knew the score: getting pinged is part of the
job.

PEASANT: Not by my own side! I appeal to you, as your fellow
man, your mother's son, your brother: have mercy.

PARA: Sorry, son. It's more than my job's worth. Now do me a
favour. Kneel.

PEASANT: (*Kneels.*)
Land of my birth, land of my fathers.
I pledge to thee my little life.
In the name of Queen and Country,

in the certain hope of Victory.

(PARA *blindfolds* PEASANT. *Drumroll. Execution.*)

KING: (*Holds up head.*) Lo, there is the end of traitors!

(*In the distance, the Spanish drum.*)

KNIGHT: It's off! It's off! The dagos are coming, mob-handed!

KING: There is plenty of time to win this game
and to thrash the Spaniards too.

(*He rolls the head along the floor. Fanfare.*)

CHORALE: God Save the Queen!

(*The* QUEEN – [PARA] – *is carried on in all her glory.*
Purposely, a man dressed as a woman.)

QUEEN: Rejoice.

CHORALE: Gloriana, Virgin Queen,
we pledge to thee our fealty.

QUEEN: Loyal subjects,
I know I have the body of a weak and feeble woman, but
I have the heart and stomach of a king, and of a king of
England too; and think foul scorn that Parma or Spain, or
any prince of Europe, should dare to invade the borders of
my realm. Let us pray, in the words of Saint Francis of
Assisi: Lord, make me an instrument of thy peace. Where
there is hatred, let me sow love; where there is injury,
pardon; where there is darkness, light; and where there is
sadness, joy. Amen.

CHORALE: Amen.

GHOST: Now cop a load of this. This is the best bit, this is.

PARA: (*Rips off Gloriana gear, to reveal Bulldog Bobby T-shirt.*)
I am the Geordie Giant
a hard man to the bone
my fist is made of iron
and my heart is made of stone.

PEASANT: (*Likewise.*)
I am a little Scallie-Wag,
a hard man to the marrow
I'll answer to my country's call
to battle royal
booze and brawl
like there is no tomorrow.

KNIGHT: (*Likewise.*)
>Beware the Brummy Bastard,
>a hard man to the core
>though Jarvis is
>a Cockney fuck
>his word to me is law.

KING: (*Retaining ancient garb.*)
>Now Scouser, Brummy,
>Cockney, Geordie –
>hard men through and through –
>who dares will win!
>I charge you men
>to do what men must do.

BILLY: (*To the audience*) You should of seen us. You should of seen us. We wasn't Millwall no more. We wasn't Liverpool or Man Ewe, West Ham or Chelsea. We was an army that day, a fucking army. We was England.

PARA: And next season we'll be kicking fuck out of each other again.

KNIGHT: Yeah.

BILLY: Friends! Brothers! Countrymen! Britons!
>I got a little proposition.
>See this here? A blue boy. Who'll take it?
>I promise you, there's a jacks in my pocket for any man who ent got the bottle for this fight.
>Straight up, all you got to do is step forward, have your money and go home. Honest to God I won't touch you.
>Any takers?
>As for them what stay, I got nothing to offer.
>Sweet F.A.
>Except bruises and cuts and broken bones,
>I can promise you that –
>the toe of a boot in the back of your neck,
>the blade in your cheek, the fist in your balls –
>you know the story.
>Who'll take five quid – a packet of fags
>and a couple of pints
>and back to your pit with a greasy slag –

87

who'll take it?
What? No takers? Not one?
You must all be mad. You must all be right nutters and
hard cunts to a man!
(*The* ARMY *cheers.*)
Lads, lads – there's ten of them to one of us.
That's appalling odds – for them.
(*The* ARMY *cheers.*)
Dear friends – there's mugs at home
in front of the box
or down the pub
or shagging their tarts
who'll kick themselves
and bite their lip
in years to come
because they was not here today
to fight with us – this crew, this fighting crew,
this band of ruckers, this England!
(*The* ARMY *cheers.*)
Are you ready for the off?
(*The* ARMY *cheers.*)
Are you all tooled up?
(*The* ARMY *cheers.*)
With pick-axe handle and baseball bat
with Stanley knife and razor blade,
hammer, bottle, chisel, wrench –
feel it, weigh it, understand it:
graft it, weld it to your arm.

And back to back we'll fight like brothers.

GET INTO 'EM! GET INTO 'EM!
(*He tears off his shirt, takes out the gun and fires at random. He
sees what he has done. Blackout.*
 *The scene is now the interior of a church. Sacred music.
Candles. A pietà.* BILLY *is alone.*)
Shadows tonight have struck more terror in my heart
than could the massed substantial ranks of Spain.

For in each darkened doorway I have passed
I thought there hung a lifeless carcass –
whose ghastly face, a speechless mask
as pale as moonlight, set with terror,
fixed my eye and froze my heart.
Each dangling limb as stiff as plyboard:
dead. As dead as firewood.

These things I thought I saw tonight
were shadows.
But, as dreams may make the brave man sweat,
so these were cast in timeless metal.
No statue will outlive that sight,
now branded on my inner eye.

For at one corner, in a rage,
I turned about and cried aloud:
Live again! For God's sake, live!
By the power which gave life to you
I beseech that murdered man
shall be released from heaven's thrall
to plough his grave into a pasture;
and Youth cut down in his high morning,
cropped in War's untimely harvest,
let him taste again the sweets
of dear and precious life;
let mothers welcome back their sons
and wives, their husbands; children, fathers.
And so enjoy his natural term
as God allows, as we may hope.
For what Almighty God has given,
he alone may take away.

Nor a whisper, nor an echo
of my own voice answered me.
I stood and looked on vacancy.

And knowing not which way to turn

I saw this church and entered here.

My conscience has a thousand voices
and every voice a tale to tell
and every tale is villainy,
gross and selfish villainy.
I am condemned a murderer.

Despair is a sin.
But I have good reason to despair.
There is no man loves me.
Nor woman, nor beast, nor insect, nor any thing.
What have I done? I have killed the world.
I am alone, and always to be alone,
to walk the earth and scratch in rubble
searching for one living thing
to speak my guilt, to beg forgiveness . . .
I shall not bear it. Sleep! bind up my wounds!
I am tired of this life.
Hush now. Say your prayers.

If I should die, let no man mark my passing.
Never fall a tear,
for not one drop of pity has ever softened me,
nor kind word, nor gentle touch.
I understand I never was
the thing I did imagine.
I am paid in full. I have my reward.

Would I were in a London pub!
I would give all my wealth,
and sacrifice my pride and fame
for a pint of beer, and safety.
Where are you, brother?
Have you abandoned me? Bobby? BOBBY?

Who will listen to my prayers?
I hate and fear the God of Wrath,

Almighty Father of the Desert.
For He has made this wilderness,
and littered it with brutish tribes.
I curse the day that I was born!
I cannot see the life to come.

O Mother Mary, pray for me.
I come to you a contrite child,
a shadow of my former self.
Take this load away from me.
Let me be at home again.
Let everything be possible.

Hail, Holy Queen, Mother of Mercy;
hail, our life, our sweetness and our hope!
To thee do we cry, poor banished children of Eve;
to thee do we send up our sighs,
mourning and weeping, in this vale of tears.
Turn then, most gracious Advocate,
thine eyes of mercy towards us;
and after this our exile, show unto us
the blessed fruit of thy womb, Jesus.
O clement, O loving, O sweet Virgin Mary.

(*Pause. Then, to the audience*) I remember that morning how
the sun come up double quick and took me by surprise.
One minute it was pitch dark, and the next . . . bingo.
    Everywhere was red fields. And a line of white windmills.
And at the edge of the plain there was mountains. Five
miles or fifty, I couldn't tell. It was like a picture I was
looking at. It was unreal. And it was just beautiful. But it
had come too late. Too late by then.
(*The light becomes diffuse. England. Winter. A park bench.*
BILLY *sits, the pram beside him.*)
    The pond's all froze up. Look at the ducks. Look at the
quack-quacks. We should of brung some bread.
    You hungry yet? You're smiling. You're smiling, ent
you? What you got to smile about?
    How about if we ran away, you and me. Eh? Where shall

we go?

I know what. I'll build you a snowman.

(CASS *walks on, wearing an overcoat, head down.*)

Cass? Cass! Is that you?

(CASS *stops, turns.*)

CASS: Oh. I didn't see you.

(*Pause.*)

BILLY: Must of been the pram, eh?

CASS: Yeah.

(*Pause.*)

BILLY: How you doing then?

CASS: All right.

BILLY: Good. Good. (*Pause.*) I'm not so bad meself. (*Pause.*) So. It's cold.

CASS: Yeah.

BILLY: You ent seen the kid, have you? You want to have a look? Go on. He won't bite you. He's already had his breakfast.

CASS: (*Peering*) Ugly little bastard.

BILLY: Takes after his father.

CASS: What's he called?

BILLY: Bobby. (*Pause.*) Cass, I . . .

CASS: Malcolm got married.

BILLY: I heard.

CASS: You didn't go then?

BILLY: No.

CASS: Me neither. (*Pause.*) How's Julie?

BILLY: She's fine. You know Julie.

CASS: Yeah.

BILLY: She was asking about you.

CASS: Uh–hu.

BILLY: Yeah.

CASS: You hear about Terry?

BILLY: No, what?

CASS: He's living up the Edgware Road.

BILLY: The Edgware Road? What for?

CASS: Job.

BILLY: Yeah?

CASS: He's a bellboy at the Inter-Continental.

BILLY: He's never.

CASS: He is.

BILLY: The jammy sod.

CASS: Yeah.

BILLY: Well, how about that then. Would you believe it.

(*Pause.*)

CASS: You been down Millwall this season?

BILLY: Nah. You?

CASS: What you think?

(*Pause.*)

BILLY: They ent won away yet.

CASS: I know.

BILLY: Typical, innit?

CASS: They want to get their defence sorted.

BILLY: That's what I always said.

CASS: I ask you. Halfway through the season . . .

BILLY: . . . and they ent won away.

CASS: Chronic.

BILLY: Yeah. Listen . . . you fancy a drink? We got some cans in.

(*Slight pause.*)

CASS: I'm working.

BILLY: What? On Christmas Day?

CASS: Yeah. Hard old life, innit? I got a job at the hospital. Porter.

BILLY: Oh . . . well . . . maybe . . . I mean . . . tomorrow? . . . if . . .

CASS: Tomorrow?

BILLY: Julie'd love to see you.

CASS: OK.

BILLY: Yeah?

CASS: Yeah.

BILLY: Right. Good.

CASS: See you, then.

BILLY: See you, Cass. Mind how you go.

(CASS *goes*.)

(*To the baby*) See who that was? Uncle Cass. Uncle Billy

and Uncle Cass. Say uncle, go on. Uncle. Oh well, never mind. You'll soon catch on. The world is full of uncles.

(*He gets up and, very slowly, pushes the pram away. Christmas music starts: 'God rest ye merry gentlemen'.*)

We'll go home now. Have our din-dins. Open our prezzies. I wonder what I got you, eh? I wonder what it is. Ent you excited? I am. I am. Come on. We're going home, Bobby. Bobby: we're going home.

(*Christmas music fills the theatre as the play ends.*)

SMALLHOLDINGS

For Maureen Glackin

CHARACTERS

AILISH – 17 years old
KATHY BYRNE – 19 years old

Smallholdings was first performed by the Loose Exchange Theatre Company at the King's Head Theatre, Islington, London on 21 July 1986. The cast was as follows:

AILISH	Maureen Glackin
KATHY BYRNE	Helen Anderson
Director	Nigel Halon
Lighting	Jenny Pullar
Sound	Paul Arditti

In April and May 1941, Belfast was bombed four times, twice daily. The shelters were probably fewer and worse than in any other British city. A hundred thousand trekkers, or 'ditchers' as they called them, fled to the countryside after the first big raid. *Smallholdings* is set on a hill farm near the border between Fermanagh and Donegal in early 1945.

SCENE ONE

A hilltop. Tree stump. A few mossy stones around its base. 'Caitlin Triall' played on a pipe. The pipe is joined by a bodhran as the lights come up to show AILISH *dancing. She is watching her feet.* AILISH *continues dancing as the music fades away. She sings the tune to herself as she dances. Suddenly she stops and listens.*

AILISH: Georgey?

> (*She backs off to one side of the stage.*)
> Georgey?
> (KATHY *enters at the other side. They look at each other.*)
> Who're you?

KATHY: Sure I'm no friggin' Georgey for starters. What aboutcher? Jeez you're a wild wee dancer. Aye. Dainty floatin' steps. And here am I in cloggy boots and feet like mud. Walk bloody walk till me bloody legs break. (*Spits.*) Ach, that's a steep climb up here. Worth it for the view though, eh? Aye. (*Looks out and takes a deep breath.*) Now would that be the Free State down there?

AILISH: Who are y'?

KATHY: Ach, where's my manners? Sure I've been so long walking I've forgotten how to be a lady. I'm Kathy Byrne and by Christ I'm knackered. What aboutcher?

AILISH: This is my father's hill.

KATHY: And this is my mother's arse. (*Sits down on the stump.*) Aah! Now what I could do with a dirty great hunk o' soda bread. And a walloping pair o' sausages. A brave big fried breakfast straight out the pan, oh God I can smell it now. I can, I can smell something frying, I swear I can. Can you smell it?

AILISH: No.

KATHY: Coming from that wee house down there.

> (AILISH *does not respond.*)
> I've had a bad winter. Nothing to eat but blackberries and raw spuds for the last three months. I can't sleep for the cramps. I can't walk for the squits. Is that your wee house?

(AILISH *does not respond*. KATHY *stands*.)

I'm a hard worker so I am, better 'n a land girl. I can plant and lift spuds, I can hoe drills, I can top and tail turnips, I can bale wheat and thresh it. I can chop wood. I can milk a cow. And I can drive a tractor. I'll give you a whole day's work for one fried breakfast. How's that?

(AILISH *does not respond*.)

What d' y' say?

AILISH: No. We're not hiring.

KATHY: Please.

AILISH: Y' must go now.

KATHY: For pity's sake, a scrap of bacon . . .

AILISH: Away out o' here, this is private property!

KATHY: Private property, is it?

AILISH: Aye.

KATHY: Sure I've walked every yard of this bloody green country from the Shankill Road to County Fermanagh. And it's a rare pretty ould land to my eyes. But every last inch of every blasted field belongs to some bastard with a shotgun. Sure, isn't there a war on? And it's the *German* army we're shooting at now, Seamus.

AILISH: (*Flares.*) D' you call me Seamus?

KATHY: And d' you call me Georgey?

(AILISH *is brought up short*.)

Aye. Georgey.

AILISH: (*Quickly*) You're trespassing.

KATHY: Now might that be the name of a man, by any chance?

AILISH: I'll call my brother. He'll kick you down this hill.

KATHY: Arrah, whisht, now! I can keep a secret.

AILISH: I'm going for my brother.

KATHY: (*Cuts her off.*) I'll beat the tripes outa you first! (*Raises her fists.*) I know how to use these. I'll take on the both o' youse.

AILISH: Niall!

KATHY: That's right. Cry away.

AILISH: Niall!

KATHY: But Christ I'll tell.

AILISH: Niall! What will you tell?

KATHY: A–ha.
AILISH: (*Without conviction*) Niall.
KATHY: Fight your own battles.
AILISH: I can't fight.
(*Beat.* KATHY *sighs and drops her stance.*)
KATHY: No more can I. No more can I. (*Sits.*) God give me strength for I've none of my own. Your brother's slow coming.
AILISH: Aye.
KATHY: He's away to the market the day.
AILISH: (*Beat.*) How did you know?
KATHY: I seen a man on the road, driving pigs. Don't be scared, I couldn't scratch a flea. I'll just sit a while.
(*Slight pause.*)
AILISH: Are you a tinker?
KATHY: Don't be calling me no tinker! Damn the lot of yez, I'm no damn tinker! I hate tinkers. They beat me with sticks and all I done is beg a ride. (*Slight pause.*) They call me a ditcher. A ditcher. I sleep in ditches . . . I used to live in a house, the same as you. Ach, *I* know who I am.
(*Pause.*)
AILISH: If I give you to eat will you go?
KATHY: What've you got?
(AILISH *pulls a hunk of bread from her bag-apron.*)
AILISH: There.
(KATHY *grabs the bread and tears into it.* AILISH *watches her eat. In the distance, the sound of an approaching aircraft.*)
A ditcher.
KATHY: Aye.
AILISH: Did you come far the day?
KATHY: Aye. Omagh. And seen not a soul on the road. Sure it's the badlands out here.
AILISH: I've never been to Omagh.
KATHY: Omagh. Strabane. Londonderry. Coleraine. Ballymena. Antrim. (*Beat.*) Belfast.
AILISH: Belfast?
KATHY: Aye. That's me. Born and bred.
AILISH: Where's your people?

(*Pause. The aircraft is close.*)

KATHY: I've none.

(*The aircraft is directly overhead.* AILISH *looks up and watches it pass.* KATHY *does not raise her head from eating.*)

AILISH: Will you look at that! (*Waving*) Hall–oo! What a lovely thing! Imagine flying. Imagine it. How do they ever come down?

(KATHY *stops eating but does not raise her head. As the noise dies away the lights fade.*)

SCENE TWO

The same. Moonlight. KATHY *is curled up by the tree stump.*
AILISH *comes in with a folded blanket.*

AILISH: (*Blindly*) Hello?

(KATHY *springs to her feet.* AILISH *recoils with a sharp intake of breath.*)

KATHY: Who's there?

AILISH: It's me. I was here before. I gave you food.

KATHY: Come where I can see y'.

(AILISH *moves. Slight pause.*)

Where's your brother?

AILISH: In the house. (*Slight pause.*) I brought you a blanket. I thought y' might be cold.

(*Slight pause.*)

KATHY: Oh.

AILISH: There.

KATHY: Oh. A blanket. That's . . . I . . .

AILISH: I'll go back now, before I'm missed.

KATHY: No. Don't go. (*Pause.*) It's a wild moon tonight.

AILISH: Aye.

KATHY: Your brother's back from the market, then?

AILISH: Aye.

KATHY: And did he sell the pigs?

AILISH: No. If he'd sold the pigs y' could come down to the house. He's in a bad temper. I daren't speak.

KATHY: Sure it's a mild night. I've known worse.

AILISH: You've the blanket.

KATHY: Aye. It's wool. I won't steal it. I promise.
(*Pause.*)

AILISH: Well. I must go now.

KATHY: What's your name?

AILISH: Ailish.

KATHY: Ailish. That's a pretty name.

AILISH: Is it?

KATHY: Aye.
(*Pause.*)

AILISH: I'm sorry I called you a tinker.

KATHY: Ach . . .

AILISH: Y' came on me so sudden like. And y' talk so wild.

KATHY: And you was expecting company.

AILISH: Maybe.

KATHY: Aye. A man.

AILISH: Who sez?

KATHY: D' y' think I was born yesterday? (*Slight pause.*)
Georgey, that's an English name. Is he a soldier-boy?

AILISH: It's none of your business.

KATHY: Right enough. Me and my big mouth. I talk a lotta ould
shite sometimes. (*Slight pause.*) No offence, then?

AILISH: No.

KATHY: (*Spitting on her palm, holding out her hand*) Shake.
(*They shake hands.*)
I've a mind to head for the Free State the day.

AILISH: Oh. Well then. You go that way.

KATHY: Aye.

AILISH: Good luck.

KATHY: Goodnight.
(AILISH *goes.* KATHY *watches. Then she leaves the blanket
folded and lies down. Silence. Blackout.*)

SCENE THREE

The same. Morning. The blanket is folded. KATHY *is not there.*
AILISH *enters carrying a large tin mug. She stops and looks. She*

105

sighs. KATHY *enters, rearranging her dress.*

KATHY: Morning.

AILISH: Oh. I thought y'd gone.

KATHY: No. I had to piss. Is that for me?

AILISH: Aye. It's tea.

KATHY: Good 'n' strong, I hope.

AILISH: Best drink it down quick, it'll be getting cold by now.

KATHY: (*Gulps some tea and blenches.*) Sure that's a wild mug o' tea.

AILISH: Is it too strong for you?

KATHY: No no, that's fine. I like it strong.

AILISH: The milk's fresh this morning.

KATHY: Aye. Lovely. (*Drinks.*) I can milk a cow, did I tell you?

AILISH: Aye.

KATHY: Aye.

AILISH: But that's goat's milk in your tea.

KATHY: Goat's milk, is it?

AILISH: Aye. From the nanny-goat. We've no cow.

KATHY: (*Looks into the mug.*) You get milk out of a goat?

AILISH: Aye. Fresh this morning.

(KATHY *shrugs and drinks. Pause.*)

Oh.

(AILISH *reaches into her bag-apron and brings out a roll of brown paper.*)

I forgot. There's this.

KATHY: (*Unwrapping a small sausage*) A sausage! That's mighty.

AILISH: I snuck it out. It's cold.

KATHY: It's good.

(KATHY *eats and drinks.* AILISH *watches her.*)

AILISH: You're a Protestant.

KATHY: Aye.

AILISH: Mr Hanlon's a Protestant. He's the big house and the tractor. He's nice, though. We sell him the eggs left over. He's a son in the Fusiliers.

KATHY: The Fusiliers, eh.

AILISH: Aye.

(*Pause.*)

KATHY: If y' look any harder y'll burn a hole.

AILISH: Oh.

KATHY: That's all right.

AILISH: We're not used to strangers in this neck of the land.

KATHY: (*Laughs.*) Now doesn't that sound like the Wild West pictures.

AILISH: Does it?

KATHY: Sure, they're always saying that in the Tom Mixes.

AILISH: Have you seen a Wild West picture?

KATHY: Aye. Thousands.

AILISH: (*Impressed*) Y' have not!

KATHY: I have too!

AILISH: Oh, I'd love to see a picture. It must be fine.

KATHY: Aye. I suppose so.

AILISH: It must be.

KATHY: Sure I can't remember. It was a long time ago.

AILISH: Y' must remember something.

KATHY: No.

AILISH: Where y' went. Y' must remember that. Eh?
    (*Pause.*)

KATHY: The flea-pit.

AILISH: The flea-pit?

KATHY: The picture house. We . . . great white pillars . . . and coloured lights outside.

AILISH: Coloured lights?

KATHY: Aye, till the blackout.

AILISH: I'd love to see coloured lights. (*Pause.*) And what else?

KATHY: Ach, I'm no good at describing.

AILISH: Oh please.

KATHY: I can't remember.

AILISH: Sure y' can. Start from y' go in the door.

KATHY: (*Pause. Then, grudgingly*) Oh. Y' go in the door. And there's a man in a dickey to tear your ticket.

AILISH: Sure, y' pay for it first.

KATHY: Aye, aye, y' pay for it first. And y' go inside. And you sit in a red velvet seat and there's singing.

AILISH: Singing?

KATHY: Aye. Everyone sings 'God Save the King' and sometimes there's a conjurer or a man telling funny stories or a contest and more singing till the lights go out and everyone goes hush and the picture starts. And you sit in the dark . . . and you forget where y' are . . .

AILISH: Aye? (*Pause.*) Then what?

KATHY: Then everyone sings 'God Save the King' again. And y' go out in the street, the same ould street. But it's like you've been away a long time because everything looks different, everything . . . Ach, I'm no good at describing.

AILISH: Yes y' are. It sounds lovely. Like nothing else.

KATHY: Aye. It was wild.

(AILISH *sighs.*)

I'll show you something.

(*Out of an overcoat pocket she pulls a tattered old magazine.*)

It's a picture magazine. There's photographs inside, look. Veronica Lake. She's a fillum star.

AILISH: What's that she's balancing on her head?

KATHY: Sure that's a hat, so it is.

AILISH: Looks like a frying pan.

KATHY: That's very stylish. They call it a cloche. That's French for hat.

AILISH: Why's she got her shoulders sticking out like that? She looks like an omaddon.

KATHY: She does not! Sure you're talking like an ould biddy.

AILISH: (*Flaring*) An ould biddy, is it now?

KATHY: Lookit. Them's shoulder pads. They give her a tapered figure. Tiny wee waist, y' see?

AILISH: Oh. Aye.

KATHY: Jeez, you've a temper on y'.

AILISH: (*Reading*) '. . . the hair hanging just on to the shoulder and curled inwards to form a roll. The front off the forehead, with side parting.'

KATHY: She's very pretty, isn't she?

AILISH: Aye. (*Hesitates, then*) D' y' think . . .

KATHY: What?

AILISH: . . . am I pretty?

KATHY: (*Looks at her.*) Has he not told y', then? Has he not said?

(AILISH *looks away.* KATHY *grabs her chin and pulls her*

back.)

Let's have a look at y'.

(*She turns* AILISH'*s face from side to side, to see her profile*.)

Aye. Aye. How old are y'?

AILISH: Nearly 18.

KATHY: (*Letting go*) There's hope yet.

AILISH: D' y' think so?

KATHY: Is he very handsome?

(AILISH *looks away*.)

Aye, you're pretty as a sweetpea, sure enough. But you're too shy to make a woman. There's one or two things I could teach y'. (*Slight pause*.) I could do with a wash.

(*Blackout*.)

SCENE FOUR

A music tape plays forties dance music, which fades as the lights come up to reveal KATHY *and* AILISH *dancing*. KATHY *leads.* AILISH *is uncertain*.

KATHY: Do you come here often? Don't look at your feet. Just follow me.

AILISH: Oh aye . . .

KATHY: Do you come here often? (*Slight pause*.) Ailish! You're not listening.

AILISH: I'm tired, Kathy.

KATHY: D' y' want to be a gog-eyed wallflower all your life?

AILISH: No!

KATHY: And to shrivel up like a leaf? And to die alone?

AILISH: No!

KATHY: Well then. Wake up. We'll start again.

(*They dance*.)

Do you come here often?

AILISH: Aye.

KATHY: No.

AILISH: No, this is my first time.

KATHY: That's better. And did you come on your own?

AILISH: No, I came with my friend.

KATHY: You're a very pretty girl.

AILISH: Thank you.

(KATHY *puts her hand on* AILISH'*s arse.* AILISH *recoils.*)

Kathy . . .!

KATHY: It's only pretend.

AILISH: You shouldn't do that. It's not nice.

KATHY: My God. You'll be safe, anyway. Come back. I won't touch y'.

(*They dance.*)

There.

(AILISH *giggles.*)

What is it?

AILISH: What you did.

(*Pause.* AILISH *grabs* KATHY'*s arse and squeezes it.* KATHY *squeals.*)

KATHY: Leave my bum alone.

AILISH: And you leave mine.

KATHY: Pax.

AILISH: Pax.

KATHY: You're not so shy.

(*They dance.*)

Now you say something.

AILISH: What?

KATHY: Anything y' like. Make conversation.

AILISH: How?

KATHY: Jeez, ask him a question. He'll talk about himself.

(*Pause.*)

AILISH: I can't.

KATHY: Sure y' can.

AILISH: I've no call asking questions. It's stupid.

KATHY: Try.

AILISH: Sure, this is daft. When will I ever go to a dance, anyway?

KATHY: After the war. Sure, there'll be dances then. Imagine it, Ailish. All those men. (*Slight pause.*) What's the matter?

AILISH: Nothing.

KATHY: Why are y' sad?

AILISH: I'm not. I'm not.

KATHY: Then will I fetch y' some punch?

AILISH: I don't mind. I prefer champagne.

KATHY: Oh is that so? Boys, did y' hear that? The lady prefers champagne.

AILISH: My father's the Earl of Kilkenny.

KATHY: Her father's the Earl of Kilkenny, so he is. Aren't you warm in that?

AILISH: No.

KATHY: Jeez, but it's hot in here.

AILISH: Then take off your jacket.

KATHY: Oh and aren't you the smart one?

AILISH: I'm smart as a fart and twice as whiffy.

KATHY: Oh–ho. And will y' take a walk outside?

AILISH: If you like.

KATHY: No, no, no, no, no.

AILISH: Oh.

KATHY: Never, never, never go outside. Never in a million years. He'll have your back to the wall before y' can draw breath. And grinding y'. And slobbering over y', and grasping at y' . . . Men can be pigs, Ailish, when they've got the smell of y'. One thing they want.
(*Pause.*)

AILISH: And is that all there is? Kathy?

KATHY: Sure, I don't know. (*Slight pause.*) It's the ones in uniform that is now. They're the worst. Ach, they're frightened is all. They go at you like they're drowning. (*Slight pause.*) Is Georgey . . . is he a soldier? (*Pause.*) I thought so. (*Slight pause.*) How well d' y' know him?

AILISH: Well enough.

KATHY: Y' see . . . I knew a girl, a girl at home. And she walked out with a soldier. He was a corporal too. Such a sweet boy, such warm eyes. Everyone liked him and she loved him well. And do you know what he did? The night before he's gone to France, he grabs her – this girl – and he says, 'You've got to. I'm going to die, you've got to.' Well that's a man for y'.

AILISH: And did she?

KATHY: Aye. She did. She did. Up the alley, where the whores

go. (*Slight pause.*) Well I hope they got him. I hope the
Jerries got him. (*Slight pause.*) Ach, liven up, girl. Forget
the war. They're playing the polka. Would y' care to dance?

AILISH: No. Stuff your dancing.

(*Blackout.*)

SCENE FIVE

The same. KATHY *sits on the stump, brushing the knots from her
hair. A tractor can be heard in the distance.* AILISH *comes up with a
small mirror.*

AILISH: I found it.

KATHY: Who's that in the tractor?

AILISH: Mr Hanlon. Here. Let me.

(AILISH *takes over brushing* KATHY's *hair.*)

KATHY: Ow!

AILISH: Keep still. I won't hurt y'.

(*Pause.*)

KATHY: I could walk down this hill. I'd be in another country.

AILISH: Aye. And will y'?

KATHY: Sure, I don't know. Both sides look the same to me.
Wee fields.

(*Pause.*)

AILISH: Y' see that ould clachan down there in the Free State?

KATHY: Aye.

AILISH: I went to school there. And that spire, that's our
church. How far, d' y' reckon?

KATHY: One mile. Two.

AILISH: Not at all. It's twelve, since they closed the border. For
a farmer going south to sell his cows it's a day's journey
now. Aye. The soldiers closed the road, so they did. One
day they come with the big oil drums. Well, my Da went
down with Mr Power and Mr Mahon and Mr Hanlon and
rolled the drums away. So the soldiers come back with
pick-axes and put craters in the road. And the farmers went
down – ten of 'em, that time – they went down with gravel
to fill in the holes. And the soldiers come back with

dynamite. And they blew up the bridge. (*Pause.*) We used to have a market. And a dance on market day. Sure, they killed the town stone dead. Where the road ends by the blowed-up bridge, it's a rubbish dump now. Sure it's no life here.

(*The sound of one or two distant gunshots.*)

KATHY: What the hell's that?

AILISH: That's Niall, shooting rabbits.

KATHY: Oh.

AILISH: He says y' can come down to the house. I'll make you a bed on the floor. (*Finishing, she stands back.*) There. Now y' can look at yourself.

(*She picks up the mirror and gives it to* KATHY. KATHY *looks in the mirror. Very long pause. Blackout.*)

SCENE SIX

The same. AILISH *is crouched behind the tree stump. Scattered in front of the stump are some pieces of linseed cake.* AILISH *puts a last handful on top of the stump, then waits and watches.*

KATHY: (*Off, calls*) Ailish!

AILISH: Ssh!

(KATHY *enters with a sack.*)

KATHY: Sack.

AILISH: Good. Now get down on the ground and keep still as y' can.

KATHY: What for?

AILISH: Will y' do as I say?

(KATHY *lies down on her stomach, propping her chin on her hands.*)

KATHY: What's that stuff?

AILISH: Linseed cake.

KATHY: What're y' gonna do?

AILISH: Wait and see, Kathy Byrne. And keep your mouth shut if y' can. (*Smiles.*) It's the funniest sight, I promise y'. (*Pause.*) Here he comes.

KATHY: Is that all? A bloody squirrel?

AILISH: Ssh.

KATHY: I've seen a bloody squirrel before today.

AILISH: There's more to come. You'll see.

(KATHY *shuts up for as long as she can*.)

KATHY: Sure he's a sweet wee creature though, isn't he? All eyes.

AILISH: There. He's off.

KATHY: Ach, did I frighten him?

AILISH: No. He'll be back in a while. Wait and see. It's the funniest sight. (*Pause*.) There!

KATHY: Another one. Two of 'em!

AILISH: Y' see? They must talk to each other.

KATHY: Sure, isn't that wild? Look at them sweet things.

AILISH: They're so stupid. It works every time.

KATHY: That's wonderful, Ailish.

AILISH: That's our supper.

KATHY: What?

AILISH: (*gingerly raising a small wood-chopping axe over the stump*) Squirrel stew.

KATHY: What're y' . . . NO!

(*She leaps up and chases the squirrels off*.)

Away out o' here, go 'way, y' stupid wee friggers! Shoo!

AILISH: (*Stands*.) Kathy!

KATHY: Jeez!

AILISH: What did y' do that for?

KATHY: Eh?

AILISH: What did y' do that for, y' damn eejot? You spoiled everything.

KATHY: I thought it was a game.

AILISH: That was our supper.

KATHY: I didn't know. I thought it was a game. Y' should have said. I wasn't ready.

AILISH: Ach.

(*She digs the axe into the stump. Slight pause*.)

KATHY: Do it again. Come on. Give me the axe.

AILISH: No.

KATHY: Give me the axe. I'll show y'. (*Takes the axe*.) It's heavy, isn't it? Jeez, y' must think I'm soft. I'm not,

114

though. I seen a farmer drowning puppies. In a bucket.
Holding them under with his hands. And I didn't look
away. I watched all the time. Where are they?

AILISH: It's too late, Kathy. They've gone. You've the one
chance and that's that.

KATHY: Oh. I didn't know.

AILISH: Now let's see. There's turnips in the house. And spuds.
I can boil the turnips. And I can boil the spuds. Niall's
always hungry.

KATHY: You did it on purpose.

AILISH: Eh?

KATHY: Didn't y'?

AILISH: No.

KATHY: Yes y' did. To make a fool of me.

AILISH: No!

KATHY: To make a fool of me.

AILISH: No!

KATHY: Then why did y' do it?

AILISH: I thought y'd be pleased! I thought y'd be pleased,
that's all. I wanted to show you what I do. It was stupid.
Just forget it. Jeez, Kathy, what's the matter with y'?
(*Blackout.*)

SCENE SEVEN

The same. AILISH *is sitting alone on the stump, quietly crying. In
her lap is a letter.* KATHY *enters holding a blue flower.* AILISH *looks
away.*

KATHY: (*Stands a moment before speaking.*) I turned the cabbage
drills. Damn that hoe. My hands are sore. (*Slight pause.*)
Blue is my favourite colour. D' y' have a name for this
flower?

AILISH: Wild hyacinth.

KATHY: Wild hyacinth. (*Inhales deeply.*) By Christ have you
smelt the perfume on it? It's just gorgeous.

AILISH: I know.

KATHY: Remember what I told y'. A man'll go mad when he

115

smells your skin. Never let him too close or he'll be sniffing round you like a dog. Shall I stick this in some water?

AILISH: What for? It's dead.

KATHY: Is it?

AILISH: Y' shouldn't pick that kind. They'll die soon as y' hoik 'em up.

KATHY: Oh. I didn't know that.

AILISH: (*Sharp*) No, you didn't, did y'.

KATHY: Sure it's only a flower, Ailish.

AILISH: Aye, aye, that's all.

(*Pause.*)

KATHY: Feels like summer today.

AILISH: The weather's out of season.

KATHY: (*Beginning to return the resentment*) Aye well I'm *glad* it is. Couldn't stand another morning waking up to a grey sky. I *like* it blue.

AILISH: It's out of its own season.

KATHY: Well, I wouldn't know about that, would I? I'm just a guttersnipe.

AILISH: Aye. And a Protestant.

KATHY: Eh? (*Pause.*) Sure, I don't belong here, do I? Your brother says there's work in Enniskillen.

AILISH: Are y' going, then?

KATHY: D' y' want me to go?

(AILISH *says nothing.*)

Ailish.

AILISH: I won't stop y'.

KATHY: Aye, well. I know where I stand in a town. (*Hesitates.*) Your brother says you've a letter from your Da this morning.

AILISH: Aye.

KATHY: You told me he's away working in England.

AILISH: Aye. (*Slight pause.*) He's in a detention camp.

KATHY: I know. Niall told me.

AILISH: And what doesn't Niall tell y'?

(*Pause.*)

KATHY: What's in the letter?

AILISH: See for yourself.

(*She thrusts the letter at* KATHY.)

KATHY: (*Looking at the paper*) There's nothing. It's all been
　　　scrubbed out.

AILISH: Aye. Every word. And every letter it's the same.
　　　Scrubbed out.

KATHY: Why?

AILISH: He writes the Gaelic.
　　　(*Pause.*)

KATHY: What did he do?

AILISH: He done nothing. He's no gunman, my Da. Aye, he's a
　　　hard man, sure enough. And that's why they put him in a
　　　prison. Because he's a hard man. Sure I'd love to see him
　　　again soon.

KATHY: Aye, y' will, y' will, sure y' will.

AILISH: I'm sorry for what I said, Kathy. I didn't mean it.

KATHY: Ssh. (*Pause.*) Why did y' run away from me, Ailish?
　　　Why d' y' run up here with your secrets?

AILISH: It's not you, Kathy. It's the house. I can't see the house
　　　from up here. I can see the lough. The water. Spreading
　　　out to the horizon. Kathy. Can I come with y' to
　　　Enniskillen?

KATHY: Don't be daft. Ah, sure the war'll be over soon, Ailish.
　　　And your Da'll be coming home.

AILISH: If they let him out.

KATHY: Cheer up, woman. For pity's sake give us a smile. I've
　　　told y', y' must practise smiling. Y' can frighten a man off
　　　with a smile.

AILISH: And what'll *you* do when the war's over, Kathy Byrne?

KATHY: Marry a millionaire.
　　　(*They laugh.*)
　　　Now then. How far to Enniskillen?

AILISH: Oh, why don't y' stay? Sure, I've no one else to talk to.
　　　Niall spends so much time with the pigs he's forgotten how.
　　　(KATHY *laughs.*)
　　　It's not funny. It's true.

KATHY: I don't know why I'm laughing.

AILISH: You're doolally.
　　　(KATHY *tickles* AILISH. AILISH *laughs. Pause.*)

Will y' stay?

KATHY: I came to say goodbye.

(AILISH *takes* KATHY's *hands and examines the palms.*)

AILISH: Y' must learn to hold the hoe so that no blisters come.
There is a way. I'll show you.

(*Blackout.*)

SCENE EIGHT

The same. An empty wooden wheelbarrow. A peat shovel. KATHY
lying flat on her back. AILISH *standing.*

KATHY: Jeez, I've had enough. I'm finished.

AILISH: Come on, Kathy. One more barrowload and we'll have
breakfast.

KATHY: Whose big idea was it to stick a dirty great hill between
your house and the peat-bog? Thank you, God. Sure with
faith y' can shift a mountain. But y' need arms and legs for
a friggin' wheelbarrow.

AILISH: I'll push the barrow if you'll lend a hand with the
digging.

KATHY: Ach, I don't know how.

AILISH: You'll learn. Here. (*Kneels.*) Let's see your hands.

(*She examines* KATHY's *palms.*)

You should stick 'em in a bucket o' salt water. It'll harden
the skin.

KATHY: (*Looking at her hands*) I'm gonna have a manicure after
the war. I'm gonna marry a millionaire and have a
manicure.

AILISH: On your feet, Kathy Byrne.

KATHY: (*Not moving*) D' y' know what my Da told me? You
Roman Catholic Fenian bastards, you're work-shy and bone
idle.

AILISH: Get up, y' dirty stinkin' blue-nose.

KATHY: Don't be calling me no names, y' whore, y'.

AILISH: D' y' want your breakfast or don't y'?

KATHY: Aye.

AILISH: Well then. Move.

KATHY: In a while, in a while. There's no hurry. We've all the
time in the world. (*Slight pause.*) For God's sake, sit down.
You're making me giddy.
AILISH: It's funny.
KATHY: What is?
AILISH: D' y' remember the first time y' come up here?
KATHY: Aye. (*Pause.*) What are you thinking?
AILISH: D' y' know what tonight is?
KATHY: No.
AILISH: It's the full moon.
KATHY: Is it?
AILISH: Aye. (*Slight pause.*) What are *you* thinking?
KATHY: Oh, this and that. What *about* the full moon?
AILISH: (*Shrugs.*) Just.
(*Pause.*)
KATHY: I was thinking what I told y' last night. About home
and everything. It's the first I've told anyone since. Isn't
that strange? I wonder . . . I wonder what it looks like now,
our street. I expect they'll wait for the war to end. Then
they'll start clearing . . . building. (*Pause.*) D' y' know
something? This is the longest I've stayed in one place since
then. (*Slight pause.*) I didn't dream last night.
AILISH: Kathy . . .
KATHY: Mm?
AILISH: Who'd y' like to marry in the whole world?
KATHY: Ah. So that's it.
AILISH: Go on, say.
KATHY: I don't know.
AILISH: Do y' like Niall?
KATHY: Ailish . . . !
AILISH: Well do y'?
KATHY: Sure I *like* him, but . . . well, he's your brother. I don't
. . . I don't *think* about him. Not that way.
AILISH: Oh. I just thought . . .
KATHY: Well, don't.
(*Pause.*)
AILISH: Do y' think I'll ever get married?
KATHY: Aye, sure. Everyone does. (*Pause.*) I know what you're

thinking.

AILISH: What?

KATHY: I know what you're thinking.

AILISH: What am I thinking?

KATHY: A–ha.

(*Pause.*)

AILISH: You don't know.

KATHY: I do. (*Pause.*) Ailish. You're young. There's no need to grab the first thing that comes along.

AILISH: Eh?

KATHY: Listen to me. These soldiers, they're a long way from home and they say what they like because they're not gonna be here forever. Wait for the war to end. Wait for your Da . . .

(AILISH *laughs.*)

AILISH: Kathy Byrne.

KATHY: What's so funny?

AILISH: Nothing's funny. It's . . .

KATHY: Tell me.

AILISH: Oh, Kathy, I wish I could. I wish I could tell y', but the words won't come out.

KATHY: What?

AILISH: I've got to tell someone.

KATHY: Ailish, what is it?

AILISH: I can't. I've tried and tried.

KATHY: I'll slap you.

(*Pause.*)

AILISH: His name . . .

KATHY: Georgey. I know that.

AILISH: No. That's what I call him. But it's not.

KATHY: Then what is it?

AILISH: Say Georgey.

KATHY: Georgey.

AILISH: And put an O. Georgey–O.

KATHY: Georgey–O.

AILISH: Giorgio, Y' see? It's lovely, isn't it? It's like music. Giorgio.

(KATHY *stares at* AILISH. *She is sitting up now.* AILISH *is*

slightly nervous.)
Watch this.
(*She stands and counts out her fingers.*)
Uno, due, tre, quattro, cinque, sei, sette, otto, nove, dieci.
Fingers. Dita. Dieci dita.
(*She takes off her headscarf and shakes her hair down.*)
Ecco i capelli.
(*She points to her eyes.*)
Gli occhi. Uno, due occhi.
(*She points to her nose and crinkles it.*)
Il naso.
(*She presses her finger to her lips.*)
Le labbra.
(*She puts her left hand to her right shoulder.*)
La spalla destra.
(*Then her right hand to her left shoulder, crossing her arms across her breasts.*)
La spalla sinistra.
(*She drops her arms and looks down at her body. Slight pause. Then, still with head lowered:*)
Piede.
(*She looks up, embarrassed. She smiles and executes a quick dance step or two.*)
Due piede. For dancing with.
(*Pause. She stands.* KATHY *stares.*)

KATHY: You stupid wee frigger.
AILISH: I've told no one else.
KATHY: An Eye-tie.
AILISH: He works for Mr Hanlon.
KATHY: A prisoner o' war. You stupid bitch.
AILISH: Oh Kathy, if y' saw him . . .
KATHY: It's against the law.
AILISH: Please don't be angry, Kathy. Please . . .
KATHY: What d' y' think you're doing? (*Pause.*) Why didn't y' tell me before?
AILISH: I was afraid.
KATHY: Has he . . . have y' let him . . . do anything?
AILISH: What?

KATHY: You know.

AILISH: No.

KATHY: Good. Then it's not too late.

AILISH: He's not like that.

KATHY: They all are.

AILISH: No!

KATHY: It's for your own good I'm telling y'.

AILISH: You're not my mother!

KATHY: Y' need someone to knock some sense into y'! Jeez,
Ailish, you've the mind of a child. Y' don't know anything,
do y'? Now just you listen to me . . .

AILISH: No!

KATHY: Listen!

AILISH: I won't! I hate you. I hate you, Kathy Byrne. I thought
y'd understand. But you're the same as all the rest, aren't
y'? Well, I wish I'd never told y'. I wish y'd never come to
this place. Damn you. Damn the lot of youse. You can go
to hell.

(KATHY *turns and walks.*)

Kathy.

(KATHY *stops and turns back.*)

What'll I do?

KATHY: You know.

AILISH: Y've got to tell me, Kathy.

KATHY: Forget him.

AILISH: How? I love him.

KATHY: Sure, that's a feeble woman talking. And you've to be
strong, Ailish. Trust me. (*Slight pause.*) Don't see him
again.

AILISH: No . . .

KATHY: Listen to me. Y' can do it. Y' can forget him. It's hard,
and y'll have to be strong. Listen. (*Slight pause.*) Y'll think
of him till you're tired thinking. Y'll sit down and y'll
stand up and y'll sit down again. And y'll walk around in
circles. And the days'll go on. And in the evenings y'll be
sad. And there'll be a pain, like a nail in your guts. Work.
Keep busy. That's all y' can do. And stay away from this
place. I give you three months. Then one day it'll happen.

ll wake up and y' won't love him any more. (*Slight
ause*.) And then y'll meet someone else . . .
SH: I don't want to! I don't want anyone else!
(*Pause*.)
ATHY: I'll be here.
(*Pause*.)
AILISH: It's too late, Kathy. I'm going away. He's coming for
me.
KATHY: When?
AILISH: The night. Please don't say anything.
(*Blackout. In the dark an unaccompanied tenor sings 'Torna a
Surriento'*.)

SCENE NINE

The same. Moonlight. KATHY *and* AILISH. AILISH *is dressed in her
smart Sunday clothes. She carries a sack containing a few
possessions. She is rattling off instructions.*

AILISH: The bailiff comes for the rent the first Sunday of the
month. Niall always forgets. Oh and mind y' keep him off
the booze. I know he'll set up a still soon's my back's
turned but he can't run the farm flat stinking drunk on his
back. And if the constable calls please please talk to him
nice, Kathy. Give him a cup o' tea. Strong tea, always
strong. Y' do know how t' light the fire now, don't y'?
Remember t' see you've enough firewood before dark. And
light the stove before y' go collecting eggs in the morning.
Give it plenty o' time to get going. Oh dear God, I was
gonna teach y' how to make bread. Ask Mrs Hanlon. She
knows everything. If anything goes wrong, up skirts and
run to Mrs Hanlon. Don't bother asking Niall. All he
knows is pigs. But don't let her husband talk y' down on
the price o' the eggs. He can afford it. Aye. Now you've the
planting and hoeing o' the spuds coming on y' soon. Y'll
have work enough.
KATHY: Aye.
AILISH: Aye. (*Pause*.) Kathy. Niall likes you.

123

KATHY: Aye. I know.
  (*Pause.* AILISH *paces.*)
  Are y' sure your man'll be coming for y'?
AILISH: Aye. You go in now. It's bitter out here.
KATHY: Are y' sure of him?
AILISH: He said! La luna piena. The full moon. Anyone with
  half an eye can see it. (*Looks up.*) Bright as a new sixpence.
  Not a cloud in the sky. (*Shivers.*) Sure there'll be a frost in
  the morning.
  (*Pause.*)
KATHY: What about your Da, Ailish? He's looking up at the
  moon tonight the same as you, the same moon. And what's
  in his mind, Ailish?
AILISH: I've left him a letter. He'll understand.
KATHY: He's thinking there'll be a frost in the morning.
AILISH: I wish you'd shut up with your . . . bloody friggin'
  mind-reading, Kathy Byrne!
  (KATHY *laughs. Affectionate.*)
KATHY: Aye well, at least there's one thing I've taught y'.
  (AILISH *smiles.*)
  Are we still friends, then?
AILISH: Aye. Friends.
  (*They shake hands.*)
  Will y' go in now.
KATHY: Aye, aye. In a minute.
  (*Pause.* AILISH *paces.*)
AILISH: I walked round the house this evening and counted the
  windows. I couldn't remember if it was four or five.
KATHY: And how many is it?
AILISH: Four. No, five. Oh dear God . . .
KATHY: Shall I go and see for y'?
AILISH: Don't be daft.
KATHY: Look who's talking. (*Pause.*) Have y' any money?
AILISH: No.
KATHY: And how will y' live?
AILISH: We'll get by.
KATHY: You're cracked.
AILISH: Don't say that, Kathy. (*Pause.*) This dress was my

r's. I'm the same size she was. D' y' think I've
d growing?
ure you're 18, Ailish. Y'll have wrinkles soon.
ure, I hope I don't shrink when I'm old. I hope I
't shrivel up.
: Well, did your Ma shrink?
SH: She was never old. She was . . . she died quite young. I
hardly remember her. Niall does, though. (*Pause*.) My
Granda kept geese. Isn't that funny? I'd forgot. He kept
geese, three or four. What were their names? I can't
remember. But he kept them in the yard. I can picture
them quite plain. Great white things. And they made such a
wild noise. And I could never go in the yard because of
them. That's it. I wasn't allowed. I was only wee. I wanted
to play. And one day I suppose I crept out. I remember
splashing about in a big puddle of water. And I remember
my Ma running towards me. And she gave me such a
beating . . . I hated her for years. (*Pause*.) I'm cold.
(KATHY *embraces her*.)
Kathy.

KATHY: Mm?

AILISH: D' y' like Niall?

KATHY: Well. He's quiet, I'll give him that.

AILISH: Make this your home, Kathy. Sure y've no other.
(*Pause*.)

KATHY: D' y' know what I've learned? All these fields belong to
somebody. One bastard or another. When I was a child I
used to think, all that green outside the city, y' can walk in
it, run in it, where y' want, where y' will and as far and
back again till you make yourself giddy. It's so big it must
be free, like the sea round an island. (*Pause*.)
Smallholdings. That's all there is out here.
(*Blackout*.)

SCENE TEN

The same. The next morning. AILISH *is sitting propped up against*

125

the stump. KATHY *enters carrying a large tin mug. Sligh*
before she speaks.

KATHY: I brought y' tea. Here, drink some before it ge
    (AILISH *takes the mug. She takes a mouthful and ble*

AILISH: (*Quietly*) Will y' never learn, Kathy? Let it stand
    longer. I can see my face in the bottom o' the mug.

KATHY: There's gratitude.

AILISH: It's like drinking a cloud.

KATHY: Well, give it here and I'll drink it.

AILISH: No, let me hold the mug. My fingers are cold.

KATHY: Ach, y'll have caught your death. Why didn't y' come
    back to the house? Sure, I couldn't sleep . . .

AILISH: I slept. (*Stands and looks out.*) Frost. Sure, isn't that a
    pretty sight? Like a veil. The same ould fields . . . I bet
    Georgey never saw snow. (*Pause.*) He'll be here tonight.

KATHY: Ailish . . .

AILISH: He'll be here. The full moon lasts for two nights.
    Didn't y' know that? I expect he got held up. I'd better go
    and collect the eggs before Niall misses me.

KATHY: Maybe he can't come, Ailish. Maybe something
    happened.
    (*Pause.*)

AILISH: What d' y' mean?

KATHY: Mr Hanlon came round this morning.

AILISH: What is it?

KATHY: It's over, Ailish. He told us. The war's over.
    (*Pause.*)

AILISH: No.

KATHY: It was on the wireless. (*Pause.*) It's funny. I don't feel
    any different.

AILISH: Nor do I.
    (*Pause.*)

KATHY: Ailish . . .

AILISH: It won't make any difference.

KATHY: It's over, Ailish! How many times, it's over. It was just
    the war. Don't y' see? That's all it was. And now it's over
    and there's nothing y' can do. (*Pause.*) And Georgey can go
    home now. Aye, he can go home. And he'll be free. And

row his arms around his Mammy and his Daddy.
ey'll be so happy. And he'll walk around. And he'll
eryone about y'. (*Slight pause.*) And maybe one day
come back for y'. Aye, maybe one day . . .

No. No. He'll never come back. You can't lie to me,
athy. Not you. (*Pause.*) Y' see that field? That's where I
met him. It was the harvest. I thought he'd never look at
me. (*Pause.*) So that's it, then. I can see my whole life in
front of me. I'll die here. I want to sleep. I could sleep
forever. Oh God.
(*Long pause.*)

KATHY: Don't cry.

AILISH: I'm not. Look. (*Slight pause.*) Kathy . . . we'll run
away together. You and me.

KATHY: Ach . . .

AILISH: Aye. We'll get a gypsy wagon. And a horse. And we
can plait its tail.

KATHY: And where shall we go?

AILISH: All over. Somewhere strange.
(*Pause.*)

KATHY: Your Da'll be coming home now.

AILISH: Aye.

KATHY: Aren't you happy?

AILISH: Aye. (*Pause.*) I'll tell him you're my friend. I will. I'll
tell him you're my friend.

KATHY: Go inside now, Ailish. Niall's waiting for you.

AILISH: Is he angry?

KATHY: No. No. Go along now.

AILISH: Are you coming?

KATHY: I'll just sit a while. You go in.

AILISH: I'll make the breakfast.

KATHY: Aye.

AILISH: Because you are, Kathy. You are my friend.
(AILISH *goes.* KATHY *watches. After a while,* KATHY *turns
and starts walking the other way, hands in pockets. In the
distance, a peal of church bells begins.*)